THE
CASE
OF THE
SLIDING
POOL

BY E.V. CUNNINGHAM

THE
CASE
OF THE
SLIDING
POOL

A MASAO MASUTO MYSTERY

E.V. CUNNINGHAM

DELACORTE PRESS/NEW YORK

Published by
Delacorte Press
1 Dag Hammarskjold Plaza
New York, N.Y. 10017

Manufactured in the United States of America
First printing

LIBRARY OF CONGRESS CATALOG
CARD NUMBER: 81-3221
ISBN 0-440-01114-0

For Dolly, Maxie, and George,
my Three disciples at
Laurel Way

THE
CASE
OF THE
SLIDING
POOL

1

THE SLIDING
POOL

Detective Sergeant Masao Masuto of the Beverly Hills
Police Force was a Zen Buddhist, which meant that he
was willing to accept his karma and his fate perhaps with
as much resignation as any man might hope for. But on
this day he rebelled. His fate, he felt, had become intolerable.

He was the victim of one of the many legends that
abound in southern California. This particular bit of
folklore held that it did not rain after the tenth of March,
whereupon Masuto had scheduled a long awaited and
long overdue week of vacation time to begin on the
twelfth of March. The rains began in November, as they
frequently do in southern California, and for the next
several months it rained intermittently and at times con-
stantly. On the twelfth day of March it rained, and for
the next six days it rained. It rained with fury and anger,
as it had all winter. Hillsides turned into mud and slid

down upon houses and roads; houses left their foundations and were engulfed in mud, and the dry, concrete-lined flood channel, which was euphemistically called the Los Angeles River, became a roaring torrent of white water.

Masuto's beloved rose garden, which contained forty-three varieties of rare and exotic roses, and which was enclosed by a wall of hibiscus and night-blooming jasmine, and where he had planned to spend at least one full day nurturing and pruning, became a sodden bog, and his own small and treasured meditation room, which he had built with his own hands, developed four separate leaks, so spaced as to make proper meditation impossible.

These two blows of fate were dealt to Masuto. What of his wife, Kati, and his two children—his daughter, Ana, who was nine years old, and his son, Uraga, who was eleven? Instead of the picnic at Malibu, the bicycle day on the path at Venice Beach, and the day to be spent at Disneyland, they were all cooped up, day after day, in their cottage in Culver City. Even though Masuto and his wife, Kati, were Nisei, which means that they were born in the United States of Japanese parentage, they had raised their children in the Japanese manner—whereupon neither Ana nor Uraga complained, as American children might well have done. And this only served to increase Masuto's frustration and unhappiness.

On the final day of his aborted vacation, at his wits' end for varieties of indoor amusement, Masuto produced his game of *go*. For those unfamiliar with the ancient Japanese game of *go*, it can only be said that it defies the Western mind and makes chess appear absurdly simple. According to Japanese tradition, the game of *go* was

2

devised by the Emperor Yao in the year 2350 B.C. The true *go*—not the Western simplifications which Masuto would not tolerate in his home—is played on a board that is divided into squares by 19 vertical and 19 horizontal lines. This results in 361 intersections. Each player has 181 pieces with which to play, and the play proceeds in a manner which can conceivably be taught but hardly described.

Now, on this last day of Masao's vacation, Masuto was trying to entice Uraga into a game of *go* when the telephone rang. Perhaps providentially, for Uraga frequently won at *go*, and a defeat by his son would not at this moment have raised Masuto's spirits. Kati answered the phone and then came into the living room and informed Masuto that his boss, Captain Wainwright, chief of detectives on the Beverly Hills police force, would like to speak to him.

"Tell him I'm on vacation," Masuto said sourly.

"He knows you are on vacation. He is apologetic. But he would like to talk to you, Masao."

Masuto went to the telephone and listened as Wainwright sympathized. "I know what a pain in the ass this weather's been, Masao, and the last thing in the world I'd do would be to break in on your vacation time if it wasn't raining. But I told myself you're bored as hell, and this is your thing."

Which was Wainwright's delicate way of announcing a homicide. There was no homicide squad as such on the Beverly Hills police force. With almost two dozen plainclothes detectives in a city of not much more than thirty thousand inhabitants, there was no need for a permanent homicide detail. There were simply not enough murders,

3

but when homicide did occur, Masuto and his partner, Sy Beckman, took over.

"If you're interested?" Wainwright added.

Masuto glanced into the living room, where his son stared bleakly at the go board. "I'm interested," he said, "providing I get an extra day next time."

"Good. We're up at Forty-four hundred Laurel Way. Take an umbrella. It's raining like hell."

As if Masuto didn't know.

Kati did not try to dissuade Masuto—at this point it was a relief to have him out of the house; but she made him wear a raincoat and take an umbrella as well, and she kissed him and clucked sympathetically over the mess his vacation had been. "Take care of yourself, please, Masao." But that was always on her lips when he left.

Driving north from Culver City across Motor Avenue to Olympic Boulevard and then to Beverly Drive, Masuto reflected on the fact that he was delighted to be back at work. He had once read somewhere that vacations are for amateurs. Could it be that he had lost the ability to enjoy anything but his work? Did he love being a policeman to that extent, or was it the puzzle, the question, the deeply mysterious and always disturbing problem of crime? Crime encapsulated the general illness of mankind, and as a Buddhist he was involved with mankind. Well, let that be as it might; it was a question he had turned over in his mind a hundred times. Answers were simple, so long as one did not dwell on the question.

Laurel Way—not to be confused with Laurel Canyon Drive, which is in Hollywood—is a Beverly Hills street that winds up into the Santa Monica foothills, a left turn off Beverly Drive just north of Lexington. The street follows the lip of a curving, ascending ridge, and the expensive houses on either side of the roadway overlook two canyons, one on either side of the ridge. Now, in the pouring rain, the road had become a shallow stream, and Masuto drove carefully, pleased that his old Datsun dealt so well with the elements; this was a day for elements. Forty-four hundred was a sprawling, stucco-covered, single-story house. There was just room in the driveway to park his car between Wainwright's Buick and a city prowl car.

As Masuto climbed out of his car and opened his umbrella, Detective Sy Beckman appeared on a path that seemed to circle the outside of the house. Beckman, a huge man, six feet three inches and built like a wrestler, grinned sympathetically. "It never rains but it pours," he said. "Me, I take my vacation in the summertime."

"Thank you. Now what have we got here?"

"Come and see. This one's a doozy."

He followed Beckman along the path, around the side of the house, through an alley of rain-soaked acacia to the terrace behind the house. It was a lovely terrace, about sixty feet long, paved in red brick, decorated with a·proper assortment of palms and jasmine, with a splendid view of hills and canyons descending to the city below, and with a space in the center for a swimming pool. But the swimming pool was gone, and with it a goodly part of the terrace, leaving a gaping hole, or rather a three-sided gap in the outer rim of the terrace. Moving gingerly, Beckman led Masuto to where the outer edge of the terrace still survived, an iron railing originally placed there as a safety precaution. Where the hole was, the railing had been torn away. Now, leaning over the rail-

5

ing, Masuto saw the swimming pool sitting halfway down the canyon side, a wide gash in the mesquite marking its journey from its original position.

"Nothing like a little rain in Los Angeles," Beckman said. "Full of surprises."

"Masao, is that you?" Wainwright shouted.

He was in the hole left by the ambulatory swimming pool, and with him, in rain hat and raincoat, was Dr. Sam Baxter, the part-time medical examiner of Beverly Hills. There were not sufficient homicides in Beverly Hills to warrant a staff medical examiner. Baxter, chief pathologist at All Saints Hospital, doubled as medical examiner when needed.

"Get down here, but do it carefully," Wainwright told him. "I wouldn't give you twenty cents for the rest of this terrace."

Masuto folded his umbrella and let himself down into the hole that had contained the swimming pool. Beckman followed. The rain was tapering off, and in the distance, over the Pacific, the clouds were breaking apart, revealing gashes of blue sky.

"Now that your Oriental wizard has arrived," Baxter said sourly, "I'd like to go. Never should have been here in the first place."

Masuto had resigned himself to being ankle deep in mud, but the bottom of the hole was quite firm, the water having drained down into the canyon. Actually, the excavation was in that peculiar soft rock which characterizes most of the Santa Monica hills and which is called, locally, decayed granite; and while the force of the constant winter rains had loosened the pool, over-filled it and weakened its supports to send it finally sliding down into the canyon, most of the ground it had once rested on was intact and firm, sloping from the shallow end to the deeper part. Wainwright and Baxter stood in the middle section. Masuto joined them. Wainwright pointed at the ground in front of them.

"There it is, Masao."

From the terrace a uniformed policeman called out, "The ambulance is here, captain."

"We'll be through in five minutes."

"Can I go now?" Baxter demanded.

Masuto stared silently and thoughtfully at what Wainwright had pointed to. A groove about six feet long, two feet wide and a foot deep had been gouged out of the dacayed granite upon which the pool had rested. The groove was half full of muddy water; the rest of the water apparently had been bailed out with a plastic pail that stood nearby. Lying in the water that remained, there was a human skeleton.

"Well, go ahead, ask me!" Baxter snorted. "Ask me what killed him and how long he's been dead!"

"I wouldn't dream of asking you that," Masuto said mildly. "You said 'he.' It's a man, I presume?"

"It was, and that's all I know. When we pick up the bones and get them back to the lab, I may know more and I may not. Have you seen enough, or are you going to stand there gawking at it all day?"

"I've seen enough," Masuto said.

"Then I'm going."

Wainwright thanked him.

"For what? For getting a case of pneumonia?" He stalked over to the shallow end of the pool and climbed out. "Get all the bones," he snapped at the two ambu-

7

lance men, who were waiting with their basket. "And don't mess things up."

"Lovely man," Beckman said.

"Where are the owners of the house?" Masuto asked.

"Inside. Nice people. They're a bit shaken. Bad enough to lose a swimming pool—a skeleton under it doesn't add to the pleasure."

"No, I suppose not."

"You talk to them, Masao. See what you can pick up about this. The pool's been here about thirty years, so I suppose we'll come up with a dead-end John Doe. Give it a shot anyway. We can't just write the poor bastard off."

The ambulance men finished collecting the bones and departed, Wainwright following them. Masuto said to Beckman, "Let's get rid of the rest of the water in there, Sy."

"Why?"

"Did they bury him naked? I wouldn't think that shoes are biodegradable. Where are they? Buttons, belt buckle, even pieces of cloth. There was nothing on the bones."

"Maybe it washed out. That was a damned heavy rain. It washed most of the dirt out of the hole."

"Let's look."

Beckman sighed, picked up the plastic pail, and began to bail. He got the water down to a level of about an inch, and then he and Masuto explored the grave carefully with their hands. There was nothing but bits of decayed granite and loose dirt.

Wet and dirty, the two men looked at each other and nodded.

"Buried naked," Beckman said.

"Which bespeaks a sense of thoroughness," Masuto decided. "It's a beginning."

"How's that?"

"First facts concerning the killer. He's a careful man, a thorough man. Doesn't like loose ends. A sense of neatness."

"Providing he's still alive. This was thirty years ago."

"Providing he's still alive. We also know he could operate a backhoe."

"How do we know that—you don't mind my asking?"

"He dug the grave. Conceivably, it could have been done with a pickax, but that would take hours. Anyway, here at the edge"— Masuto bent and touched two marks at the end of the grave —"that looks like the teeth of a backhoe. Most likely they had finished the excavation and the backhoe was still available. Maybe they planned to pour the concrete the following day. He could have come by at night, used the backhoe, cut out the grave, put in the body, and then packed it over with dirt."

"That's a lot of maybes."

"Just the beginning."

They were up on the terrace now. The rain had ended, the sky in the west was laced with pink and purple clouds that formed a curtain across the setting sun. The two men stared at it in silence for a minute or so, and then Beckman said, "There's no way we're going to break this one, Masao."

"We'll see. Let's go in and talk to the people who own the place."

2

JOHN DOE

John and Mary Kelly were the fortunate "creative" proprietors of a soap opera; fortunate in the fact that it provided both of them with enough money to live in Beverly Hills, and creative in the sense that John Kelly, a writer, had originated the soap opera—which was called *Shadow of the Night*—and Mary, an actress, was its chief running character. John, tall, stoop-shouldered, and nearsighted, had banged out the script, day in and day out for five years, and Mary, blond, blue-eyed, and pretty, had played in it day in and day out for five years. Today, being Saturday, their single day of rest, they were at home, sitting in the living room, comforting themselves with white wine and trying to adjust to the loss of a swimming pool and the ownership of a long-deceased skeleton, both in the same day. They had already spoken to Wainwright and to their public relations man and to the network—so that the latter two might

10

decide whether to make the most or the least out of these happenings—and they were now trying to make sense of their insurance policy when Masuto sounded their doorbell. John went to the door and stared with dismay at the two bedraggled men. Masuto showed his badge.

"We would like to talk to you and your wife, if we might. I'm Detective Sergeant Masao Masuto. This is Detective Sy Beckman, both of us with the Beverly Hills police force. We're wet and dirty, so perhaps we should talk in the garage."

"Absolutely not," said his wife, Mary, coming up behind him. "You poor dears. Just give me your coats and come on into the living room. We have a fire going. Anyway, nothing so exciting has ever happened to us before, and here are two in-the-flesh detectives, and John, if that isn't grist for your mill, I don't know what is."

"Right on," John agreed. "Forgive my rudeness, but you're a Nisei, aren't you? I mean, on the Beverly Hills force, that's something. I mean if we can demonstrate some sanity in Beverly Hills, it can happen anywhere, wouldn't you agree?"

"Absolutely," Masuto said.

A few minutes later, sitting in the living room and drinking hot coffee, and listening to Beckman discussing a soap opera with its creator, Masuto reflected, as he had so often before, on the wedding of the tragic and the ridiculous in his work. Beckman was explaining that while his wife never missed a segment of *Shadow of the Night* if she could help it, he only caught it on his days off. "When I tell her that we were here—well, never mind that. It's off the subject."

"Yes, of course," Kelly said. "But did you ever catch

a segment with the narc—Henderson, the narcotics squad."

"Afraid not."

"No? That's a pity. I would have appreciated a professional opinion."

"I think," the wife said, "that Sergeant Masuto would like to talk about the swimming pool."

"Oh? Oh, absolutely. You know, when I think of all the laps I've done in that pool with some poor devil's corpse right under me—sorry, go ahead."

"Just a few questions. First of all, when did you buy the house?"

"Just about four years ago, when the show got rolling. It was the first windfall Mary and I had since we married. We never dreamed we could afford a place like this."

"Captain Wainwright said you told him the pool had been there for thirty years. How did you know?"

"Just the word of the real estate agent when we bought the place. He said it had been built in nineteen fifty."

"Who owned it before you?"

"Carl Simmons. Very rich. He traded for a place in Bel-Air. He's in the plastics business in Irvine."

Beckman made notes.

"And how long did he live here? Do you know?"

"Six years, I believe."

"By the way," Masuto said, "how certain are you that the pool and the house were built at the same time?"

"Only what my real estate man told me. This was one of the first houses built on Laurel Way, and it set the pattern."

"And do you know the name of the pool builder?

Most pools have metal plates set into them with the name of the builder."

"I suppose they do, but not ours."

"You sure about that?"

"Absolutely. I was curious about it. I asked our pool-care man about it once, and he said that back in those days, most pools were not gunnite, which is a way of spraying a metal form with concrete. Ours is—or was, I should say—just an enormous concrete tub, with walls eight inches thick. That makes a great pool, but I guess it was just too much weight for the hillside to carry after the rains we've been having."

"That still doesn't explain the absence of the builder's nameplate."

"No, but our pool man—"

"What's his name?" Beckman asked.

"Joe Garcia. I have his address inside. He lives in Santa Monica. Do you want it?"

"Later," Masuto said. "Go on."

"Well, he said that probably the pool was built by the same contractor who built the house, and since he was not mainly in the pool business, he wouldn't have a nameplate."

"Do you know the contractor's name?"

"I'm afraid not."

"It was so long ago," Kelly's wife said. "Thirty years. Do you really think you could ever find out who put the body there—or even who the man was?"

"We have to try," Masuto told her.

"You can't write off a homicide," Beckman added.

"But how can you be sure it was a homicide?"

"It generally is when they hide the body," Masuto said. "But let's get back to the house. We've accounted for ten years. Do you know who the owner was before Simmons?"

"We think it was Jerry Bender, the comic," Mary Kelly said. "We still get some of his mail—can you imagine, after ten years."

"But I think he only lived here a year or two," Kelly told them.

"All right. You've been very helpful. Now I want you to think about this very carefully. In the time you've lived here, have you ever had a visit from a man you didn't know? Let me be more explicit. This man is between fifty-eight and sixty-five years old. He might have offered some excuse, perhaps that he was from an insurance company or from some city agency or from the water company—but in any case, he would be interested in seeing your terrace."

"Got you," Kelly said eagerly. "After all, I write these things. You're thinking that the killer might have come back, to see that his burial ground is undisturbed—am I right?"

Masuto smiled. "Quite right."

"The trouble is," Mary Kelly said, "that I can't think of anyone who fits that description. Can you, John?"

"Not offhand, no."

"But people do come around, I'm sure," Mary Kelly said. "The trouble is that John and I spend so much time at the studio. He has his office there, where he writes the show, and when you do a daily soap, it's very often eight or ten hours a day for me."

"And who takes care of the house?"

"We have a sweet Mexican lady, whose name is Gloria Mendoza. She comes in every day, cleans, and cooks if we come home for dinner. We give her weekends off, so she's not here today. But she'll be here on Monday."

"Perhaps we'll speak to her on Monday. Meanwhile, in a few hours you'll be besieged by reporters and media people. I would appreciate your not mentioning that either Detective Beckman or I are working on this case. If they ask you what the police are doing, you can refer them to Captain Wainwright."

When they left, Masuto informed Beckman that there was an old road at the bottom of the canyon from which they could reach the swimming pool.

"You got to be kidding. Aside from the mud, the brush is soaking wet."

"The way we look now, what difference will it make?"

It nevertheless made a difference, for by the time they reached the shell of the swimming pool, clawing up the brush-covered slope of the canyon, they were soaked from head to foot and their shoes and trousers had become soggy clumps of mud. Nor was anything to be found there, only the big concrete form, split along one side and perhaps destined to lie there on the hillside for years to come. There was no identifying plate or mark.

"Well, that's that," Masuto said.

"The hell with it," Beckman concluded. "He's been dead for thirty years, and another day or two won't hurt. Let's knock off and get into dry clothes."

With the end of the rain Kati removed the four pans she had set out in Masuto's meditation room to catch the leaks in the ceiling, thinking at the same time that she must have the roof repaired. She had heard that more

roofs leaked in Los Angeles than in any other city because the rainy season was four months long, leaving
eight dry months to lull the population into believing
that it would never rain again. Well, it would, and this
time she would make certain that the roof was repaired.

Tonight, the room was once again usable, but Masuto's
meditation was not successful. Again and again there
intruded the image of a naked man, put to death thirty
years ago. The moment he arrived home, Masuto had
telephoned All Saints Hospital, only to be informed by
the intern on duty in the pathology lab that Dr. Baxter
had left for the day. It was understandable. The bones
had kept for thirty years; they would keep for another
day. But Masuto found the puzzle compelling. He felt
that all of life was a puzzle, and most of it beyond answer.

Later, at dinner, with Masuto and his wife eating together after the children had been put to bed, Kati asked
tentatively about what horror had called him out into the
rain. Her questions were always tentative, voiced with
the understanding that the worst things would be concealed from her.

"We found the skeleton of a man murdered thirty
years ago."

"How very awful!" But with a note of relief. If it had
happened so long ago, there was surely no threat to her
husband. That concerned her most.

Masuto told her the story, stressing the fact that the
couple who owned the house were very nice people. It
was not often that he could bring Kati a story about nice
people.

"But surely there's no way you can find the killer
now?"

"We'll try."

"I'm sure he's dead," Kati said firmly. "There are other punishments beside the police."

"Possibly. In any case, we'll try."

"But not tomorrow," Kati said firmly. "Tomorrow, the man on the television tells us, will be the first sunny day in a week, and we are taking the children to Disneyland."

"I was supposed to check in," Masuto told her, but without conviction. "Today is the last day of vacation. I do not work on Sunday."

"You worked today." She had changed a good deal since she joined a consciousness-raising group of Nisei women. "You can point that out to Captain Wainwright. No one else works on Sunday."

"Except policemen."

"We are all going to Disneyland."

Masuto telephoned Wainwright, who unexpectedly admitted that the bones would keep. The Masuto family spent the day at Disneyland. And on and off, when Masuto glanced at his wife, he noted a strange, slight smile of satisfaction on her lips.

Monday morning Masuto stopped off at All Saints Hospital and made his way to the pathology room, where Baxter's two young, bearded assistants leered at him knowingly, as if every corpse sent there by the Beverly Hills police was his own handiwork. Behind them Dr. Baxter bent over the skeleton, which he had laid out on an autopsy table.

"Well, here he is," Baxter said unpleasantly, which was his normal manner. "I suppose you want his name, sex, age, and the details of what killed him?"

"Only because of my enormous respect for your skill."

"Bunk! Anyway, his name is your business, not mine."

"Very true."

"Have you got it? No. Of course not. Do you know why some murders are solved? Because murder is an idiot game. Show me a murderer, and I'll show you an IQ of ninety-five. When an intelligent man turns his hand to murder, your numbskull police force is paralyzed."

"And is that what we have here?" Masuto asked gently. "An intelligent murderer?"

"You're damn right, which is why the body stayed in its grave for thirty years. If not for these ridiculous rains, it would have remained there forever."

"Perhaps, or perhaps nothing is forever. But acknowledging that neither of us knows the name of the victim, I'm sure you can tell me the rest."

"You're damn right I can. The deceased was a male Caucasian, about five feet eight inches tall, age between twenty-five and thirty, and killed by a knife wound, a hard, deep thrust from the rear. How do I know? Come over here." Masuto took his place on the opposite side of the autopsy table. "This," Baxter said, pointing, "counting down is the sixth of the thoracic vertebrae. Notice that scrape on the left side, actually nicked a piece of the bone. Tremendous force, drove right through the vertebral aponeurosis into the heart. A long, heavy blade, maybe something like a bowie knife, back to front, right through the body and heart and nicked this rib, right here. The son of a bitch who killed him knew what he was doing. I've seen a hundred knife wounds, but not like this. This gent had practice. Nobody drives a knife through the entire thickness of a human body unless he's been trained to do it and has done it before."

"You're sure of that?"

"Was I there? I'm sure of nothing. I'm telling you what the bones say."

"How do you know it was a white man?"

"It's my guess—shape of the skull, relationships of tibia and femur, and here in the skull, the shape of the mesethmoid, right here where it holds the cartilage. Could be a black man, but not likely. Like I said, I wasn't there."

"And the age?"

"Condition of the teeth, good teeth, two missing—knocked out, I'd guess—but not one damn cavity for you Sherlocks to fool around with dental charts."

"Why do you say knocked out?"

"Because I use my head. You can see the broken stump."

Masuto ran his finger over the stump. "Worn smooth. Not a rich man. He could have had it capped. I think your conclusions are brilliant, doc."

"You're damn right they are!"

"Well, at least you don't suffer from modesty."

"Modesty is for fools. I ought to be chief medical examiner downtown, and instead I waste my years in Beverly Hills."

"What about broken bones?" Masuto asked. "Any healed fractures?"

"Not a one." He grinned at Masuto with satisfaction. "Really handed you one, didn't I? You find the man who did in this stack of bones and I'll take back every nasty thing I ever said about you."

"If he's alive, I'll find him."

"Talking about modesty—"

"As you said, it's for fools."

* * *

Wainwright was waiting for Masuto in the police station on Rexford Drive. "I suppose you've seen the papers," he said. "This city needs flashy corpses like I need a hole in my head. Would you believe it, the city manager's blaming me for a murder took place thirty years ago."

"Who else can he blame?"

"I told him to forget about it. This is a dead end. In a few days the newspapers will get tired, and we can close the file. I'm shorthanded enough without you and Beckman wasting the city's money trying to find a murderer who's maybe dead ten years ago. Especially when our chances of finding out who was zonked are practically zilch. Beckman spent half the day Sunday down at L.A. Police trying to spot a disappearance that would fit. Nothing. We got nothing, and we're likely to get nothing."

"Where's Beckman now?"

"Over with the town records. They were closed yesterday. He's trying to find out who the contractor was and when the pool was poured. But goddamnit, I know you, Masao. I don't want any federal case made of this."

"Ah, so," Masuto said mildly. "Murder is done in Beverly Hills, and the captain of detectives is indifferent. A thousand pardons, but how does one explain that?"

"Don't give me that Charlie Chan routine, Masao. I can see you licking your lips and getting set to chase ghosts for the next two months. Meanwhile, houses are being broken into and stores are being robbed."

"Will you give Beckman and me a week?"

"Why? What have you got? Bones."

Beckman walked in. He stood watching Wainwright and Masuto with interest.

"Bones that once belonged to someone, to a white man, five feet eight inches tall, in very good health, but poor, a laborer, I suspect, and truculent—oh, about twenty-seven, twenty-eight years old."

"You got to be kidding," Wainwright said.

"Who was murdered," Masuto went on, "possibly on a Sunday by his friend, a man who had commando training in World War Two, who planned the murder very carefully, and who knew how to operate a backhoe."

"And you also have an eyewitness," Wainwright said sardonically.

"An assortment of intelligent guesses put together mostly by Dr. Sam Baxter, but it's a starting point, isn't it? I'm only asking for a week. And what a feather in the cap of my good captain if we can come up with the answer."

"I'll tell you what. Today's Monday. If you can come up with a tag for the deceased and a motive by Wednesday, you got the rest of the week. If on Wednesday you still got nothing but Sam Baxter's pipe dreams, we close the file."

"You're all heart," Masuto said.

"I'm a sucker for your Oriental flimflam, that's what I am." He turned on Beckman. "Don't stand around wearing down your heels. Get in there with Masuto and do something. I got a police department to run," he said with disgust. "Crime in this city is up eight percent from a year ago, and you work on puzzles."

In Masuto's office Beckman observed that Wainwright was in a lovely mood this morning.

"Just normal good nature. What have you got, Sy?"

"I got the name of the contractor. Alex Brody on Maple Street in Inglewood. Here's the address, but whether he still lives there or is alive or dead, God knows. According to the records, the first building permit for Forty-four hundred Laurel Way was issued on May ninth, and the final inspection took place on August twelfth, both nineteen fifty. I got hold of the plans, which include the swimming pool, but there's no way of telling from the records when the pool was poured or whether it was separately contracted. If it was, it would have been a subcontract, because only one set of plans was filed."

"Was the house built on slab?"

"I thought of that," Beckman said with satisfaction. "According to the building guys they were just beginning to pour slab foundations around that time. You're thinking they would have poured the concrete for the pool at the same time."

"It makes sense. It was a slab base?"

"According to the plans."

"We'll suppose they started on May ninth, the day they got their permit. They had to put down the footings, excavate, wait for an inspection, then bring in the plumbers and lay the pipes and the ducts. It has to be three weeks to a month before they pour the concrete. Let's say the first of June—which means that our John Doe disappeared during the month of June nineteen fifty." He took a file folder from his desk and labeled it John Doe. Inside, on a sheet of paper, he wrote, "John Doe, white, age 25 to 30, height 5/8, died June 1950." He handed the file to Beckman. "There's our starting point. What did you learn yesterday?"

"From the L.A. cops—nothing. They got this new computer, and we ran through every disappearance for three years, forty-nine, fifty, and fifty-one. We turned up a lot of kids and three adult women—but nothing like an adult male. Plenty of murders, but they always managed to lay hands on a body."

"All right. I'm going to drive down to Inglewood and see if I can find the contractor. Meanwhile, check the county out with the sheriff's office, and you might as well do the adjoining counties, Ventura, Orange, and San Bernadino. Try the F.B.I. too. They keep a file on kidnapings, but I'm not sure they have one on disappearances. Anyway, check them. You might also try San Francisco and San Diego and Long Beach—"

"You don't think I'll turn up anything, do you?"

"Why do you say that?"

"If you did, you'd include every county in the state."

"And have Wainwright screaming about the phone bill?" Masuto shrugged. "Maybe you're right, but give it a try anyway. You see, I don't think this was a crime of passion, Sy. I think it was a coldblooded, planned execution. I think the killer selected John Doe because there wasn't a soul in the world who cared whether John Doe lived or died. If you want to kill someone, you kill them. It's not hard to kill a human being, and this killer was a pro. I think the killing was an adjunct to his intention and his need. His need was to make John Doe disappear—forever. That's why the body was naked."

"You'd think that with fifty thousand pounds of swimming pool on top of the body, he'd rest easy."

"No. He was or is a very thorough man. Neat, cold, calculating—and orderly. And if he's still alive, now that the body's been uncovered, he will be very unhappy, very nervous, and as sure as there's a thing in this universe called karma, our paths will cross—perhaps in the next few days."

"Come on, Masao," Beckman said, "I've seen you pull off some creepy ones, but this is way out. We may never find out who John Doe is, and now you're telling me that the killer is going to play footsie with us? How? Why?"

"All right, Sy—you tell me. Why was John Doe stripped naked? Why was he put down under the pool? Why wasn't the killer satisfied with a plain, old-fashioned murder?"

"You'll have to ask the killer those questions."

"Or perhaps not. I've wracked my brain for reasons, and I can come up with only one. It was not John Doe who had to disappear; it was our killer. And since in our very complex society it is not enough to disappear, the killer had to become someone else. He had to have a new name, a new driver's license, a new social security card, a new birth date, a place of origin and in that place, a birth certificate. He was not content with changing his name—he was too ambitious; he planned his future. He had to have a whole new identity. Do you see it now?"

"You mean, when we find out who John Doe is—"

"Exactly. We find our killer. If John Doe was twenty-eight, somewhere there's a man of fifty-nine, living with John Doe's name and credentials."

But having recited this detailed program, Masuto felt ashamed of himself. He hated a childish display of cleverness in others, and he found it intolerable in himself. The dead man did not have to be twenty-eight at the time of his murder. He could have been two or three years younger or older. That the killer needed his identity was a guess; there could be other reasons why the body had been buried naked. And would they find the killer when they discovered who John Doe was?

"He might be dead," Beckman said, too worshiping of Masuto to list other flaws in his thinking.

"Or he might be ten thousand miles away and we might discover nothing in the end," Masuto admitted.

3
MURDER
MOST FOUL

The City of New York includes five counties, and Chicago is synonymous with Cook County, whereby the belief is current that the City of Los Angeles and Los Angeles County are one and the same thing. But while the City of Los Angeles is enormous and sprawling, the County of Los Angeles is even more enormous—larger in fact than a number of European countries. Aside from the City of Los Angeles, there are in Los Angeles County dozens of other civic entities, small cities, villages, and unincorporated areas; and to make the situation even more confusing, many of these independent communities, such as Beverly Hills, Inglewood, Vernon, Culver City—to name only a few—are entirely surrounded by metropolitan Los Angeles. Each of these civic entities has its own police force, while the unincorporated areas are the domain of the county sheriff and his several thousand brown-clad deputies. No one planned this crazy quilt of authority; it just happened. And since it was Los Angeles, it happened uniquely. Yet one positive result of this weird complexity was an unusual amount of cooperation among the respective police forces, a fact which Masuto was grateful for when he found two Inglewood prowl cars parked in front of the house on Maple Street, the house where the contractor Alex Brody had once lived.

On the other hand, he had a sinking feeling of unhappy anticipation, which combined with a wave of anger against his own insensitivity, the indolence and frustration which had permitted him to spend the previous day wandering with his family through Disneyland. Even as he parked his car an ambulance swung in ahead of him, and two men with a litter got out and were ushered into the small, aged, and rather shabby house by an Inglewood cop.

Masuto showed his badge to the officer, who remarked that he was a long way from home and told him to go ahead inside. The small crowd on the street watched in silence.

Whatever Alex Brody had been, he had not been rich. The living room that Masuto walked into was neat and clean, but the cheap furniture was old, the carpet worn, the walls discolored. It was crowded with another uniformed policeman, two plainclothesmen, the two ambulance men, two frightened women who sat huddled on a worn couch, and a corpse that the two attendants were lifting onto the stretcher.

Masuto identified himself and asked to look at the corpse before they took it away.

"Be our guest," said one of the plainclothesmen. "My name's Richardson. This is Macneil," he added, nodding at the other. "What I want to know is how come a Beverly Hills cop gets here a half hour after that poor lady is killed?"

Masuto was staring at the corpse. It was a very old lady, perhaps eighty years old, with thin white hair, pale, pleading blue eyes, and savage marks on her face and head.

"She was beaten to death," Macneil said. "God almighty, what the hell is this world coming to?"

"Just two blows," Masuto said. "Crushed her skull."

"We been looking for something in the room might have done it. Nothing."

"Brass knuckles," Masuto said.

"You sure or guessing?"

"That's how she's marked." He turned away and studied the room. The two ambulance men moved out with the body. "Nothing stolen," Masuto said, more as a statement of fact than as a question.

"What's to steal? That old TV wouldn't bring five bucks at a flea market. Her bag's inside on the kitchen table. Three dollars and an uncashed social security check. I still want to know what brings you here, Masuto."

"Can we please go?" one of the ladies on the couch asked. They were both in their middle thirties, frightened, tearful.

"Just a few minutes more, ladies."

"My kids will be coming home from school."

"It's only one o'clock," Richardson said. "You'll be back home long before school's out."

"What was the old lady's name?" Masuto asked softly.

"That was Mrs. Brody, God rest her soul," one of the women on the couch said. "Never harmed no one, never bothered no one. Why do these things happen? This was once a decent place to live."

"How about it, Masuto?" Richardson reminded him.

"Let's go inside," Masuto suggested.

They sat down at the kitchen table, which was covered with a hand-embroidered blue and white cloth. A delft clock on the wall matched the cloth. The linoleum was scrubbed clean and worn through. As with the living room, the kitchen was spotless.

"Cigarette?" Richardson asked.

Masuto shook his head glumly.

"You sure as hell look miserable, Masuto. Did you know the old lady?"

"No, but she would have been alive now if I had used my head."

"You'd better explain about that."

"You read about the skeleton we found under where a swimming pool had been up in Beverly Hills?"

"I read what the papers had to say."

"Well, the man who built that pool thirty years ago was Alex Brody. We got his name and address out of the town records. I imagine that he's dead and the old lady was his widow."

"And you figure Brody for the man who put the body under the pool?"

"Oh, no. No, indeed. I think the man who put the body there is still alive, and that he came here today and he killed Mrs. Brody. It was his style. He's a man who long ago was trained to kill with his hands."

"How do you know all this?"

"Some evidence, a lot of guesswork, educated guesses."

"You got a name for him?"

"No."

"You got a name for the skeleton?"

"No."

"Seems to me you don't have a hell of a lot, Masuto."

"No, not a hell of a lot. Who are the two ladies outside? Did they see anything?"

"Maybe. Let's ask them," Richardson said. "You figure maybe Mrs. Brody knew something about her husband's business which might have led you to the killer?"

"That's why she's dead."

"Still guessing. We ain't that smart down here in Inglewood. We don't make four until we got two and two."

They went back into the living room. "They live down the street," Richardson explained. "This is Mrs. Parsons. This is Mrs. Agonian. They say they saw a man come out of the house in a hurry. They know the old lady and she don't have many visitors. So they went to the door and the door was open and they found the body."

The two women began to sniffle.

"Could you tell us something about the man?" Masuto asked kindly.

"Only from the back. We were almost a block away."

"What was your immediate reaction to him? I mean, did you feel that he was a young man or an old man or middle-aged?"

"He wasn't an old man," Mrs. Parsons said.

"He wasn't young. Maybe your age," Mrs. Agonian said, pointing to Richardson, who appeared to be in his middle fifties. "I mean that he went down the street sort of half running, you know, walking very fast."

"To his car?" Masuto asked. "Did you see a car?"

"No, he turned the corner."

"How was he dressed?"

"A business suit. He wore a gray suit."

"How tall was he?"

They both shook their heads.

"Visualize it if you can. One always has an impression of height—just your first impression. Try to remember?"

"He wasn't small."

"I think he was a big man, I mean broad, not fat, broad," Mrs. Agonian said.

"Is that all?" Richardson asked Masuto.

"I think so." He thanked the women. "You've been very helpful."

"I hope you catch him," Mrs. Parsons said. "She was a nice old lady. She never harmed a soul."

"One more thing," Masuto said. "Did she ever talk about relatives? Did she have children?"

"I don't know," Mrs. Agonian said.

"I know, I mean whatever there is to know, because she once mentioned a daughter," Mrs. Parsons told them. "But she hadn't seen her daughter for years and years. They had a terrible fight years ago when her daughter married someone she and her husband didn't want her to, and she didn't even know where her daughter was living now."

"What was the daughter's name?"

"Henrietta."

"And her married name?"

Mrs. Parsons shook her head.

"Did she have any close friends in the neighborhood?"

"Only Helen and myself. No one ever came to see her."

After the two women had left, Richardson said to

Masuto, "It don't pay to grow old, it sure as hell don't. You got all you want? We got to seal up the place. We got a guy works on fingerprints, but he's off today."

"You won't find prints. I'd like to look around. Do you mind?"

"Make yourself at home. I'll tell them to hold it open until you leave."

It was a modest house, small, in the California bungalow style, with all the rooms on one floor—living room, kitchen, breakfast room, and two bedrooms. One of the bedrooms had been converted into a kind of den and TV room; the other was used as the bedroom, and on the dresser was a picture of a young man and woman. A wedding picture. The date on it was 1922. They were an attractive couple, Masuto thought. Another photo in a small silver frame revealed a teenage girl with light hair and light eyes, smiling. Masuto went through drawers reluctantly, the worn clothing of the old lady, some child's clothes, a rag doll and some other mementos, a sad, poverty-stricken past. What had happened to Brody the contractor? What misfortune? Why this awful poverty?

Masuto was looking for records, payroll lists, tax reports. He found nothing. After half an hour of searching he gave it up and called the Beverly Hills police station. "What have you got?" he asked Beckman.

"Nothing, Masao. Absolutely zilch. June, nineteen fifty, was a lousy month for disappearances in the state of California, if you don't count lost kids. And only one of those is still missing, fourteen-year-old girl."

"What about the F.B.I.?"

"Same there. Nothing that fits in. They have a millionaire who was kidnaped in Mobile, Alabama on the sixteenth of June that year, and his body never turned up, but he was only five foot six and most of his teeth were capped. What have we got here, Masao? Can a man just walk off into thin air and disappear, with nobody putting in a complaint or a missing person?"

"It's a big country. It happens."

"What do I do now?"

"I want you to find out what services trained their men in close quarter killing during World War Two. I think the O.S.S. and the Rangers did, but there might have been others. I mean the hand-to-hand commando tactics. One thing we know about our man is that he's proficient at killing, and since that was a time when killing did not go unrewarded, he may have earned himself a bronze star or an oak leaf cluster or even a medal of honor. Who knows! So see what you can dig up. It's just a hunch, but all we got to play is hunches."

"What about Brody? Did you track him down?"

"He's dead, Sy, and an hour and a half ago, his wife was murdered."

"No!"

"Two quick blows to the head and neck. Brass knuckles. Crushed her skull and broke her neck."

"He's a real pro, isn't he?"

"When it comes to old ladies, he certainly is."

"Same address, Masao?"

"The one you dug up, yes."

"Did you find anything?"

"Nothing."

"Where are you off to now?"

"Whittier. That's were Kati's Uncle Naga has a contracting business. It's time I talked to a contractor."

But before he left the Brody house to go to Whittier,

Masuto telephoned the Los Angeles Police Department and asked to speak to Lieutenant Pete Bones, who was in homicide, whose path had crossed Masuto's a number of times in the past, and who had more than a little respect for Masuto's ability.

"What Chinese puzzle are you working out now?" Bones wanted to know.

"I'm interested in homicide."

"Oh? Anything special?"

"A killing without a gun. A knife or brass knuckles or even bare hands."

"What in hell are you talking about?"

"I'm asking you whether you've had that kind of a homicide today," Masuto said patiently.

"Why?"

"What do you mean, why? You're in homicide. You would know."

"So help me, Masuto, either you got a weird sense of humor or E.S.P. There was an old lady killed a couple of hours ago in Inglewood. We just got it from the Inglewood cops. Now what in hell are you up to?"

"I know about that. I'm sorry. I should have mentioned it. I'm calling from her house."

"What in hell are you doing in Inglewood?"

"It's a long story, and I'll give it to you first chance I get. I'm talking about another homicide with the same M.O."

"Tell me about it," Bones said angrily.

"There's nothing to tell. I'm asking you whether it happened."

"Oh, you're a doll, Masuto. You're cute. Now will you tell me what in hell you're talking about? Has someone been killed? Do you know about it? Or is someone going to be killed?"

"The latter is a possibility," Masuto agreed, forcing himself to be patient.

"Who?"

"I don't know."

"You call me up and tell me that someone is going to be killed and ask me whether it has happened yet, and you don't know who?"

"That's about it. I'm sorry I bothered you, Pete."

"Get your head examined," Bones snarled, slamming down the telephone. To Masuto, the click was more like a crash. He sighed and walked out of the house.

4
NAGA ORASHI

Naga Orashi, Kati's uncle, was among the Japanese immigrants who were rounded up and put in concentration camps during World War II. It was a shameful incident, best forgotten yet not easily forgiven, and since Naga Orashi had been brought to America at age three, he was hardly in any real sense an immigrant. By now Orashi had almost forgotten the concentration camps. Actually, though he was seventy-eight years old, he had an excellent memory, and for the most part forgot only what he chose to forget.

After the war, when he returned to Los Angeles, he built himself a cottage in Santa Monica, mostly with his own hands. By the time the house was complete his family had grown with the unexpected arrival of twins. He decided that the cottage was too small and he sold it for a substantial profit. He was then a carpenter; with the sale of the cottage he decided to become a builder and contractor, and in the years that followed he did well. His crowning achievement was to build a seventeen-story hotel in downtown Los Angeles for a group of Japanese investors. After that he turned over his building operation to his sons, content to sit on a rocking chair in the sun in the machine yard of his supply warehouse at the edge of Whittier, which is another one of the many independent towns that exist in Los Angeles County. It was there that Masuto found him, a small, wrinkled, brown-skinned man, smoking an ancient pipe and missing nothing that went on around him.

He greeted Masuto formally, if critically, explaining that "A family, Masao, is not something to be lost like rice husk in the wind. It is the fabric of mankind, even if here in this land that fact is little known and less appreciated. Where is our family? It is a year since I have seen you." He added, in Japanese, "It makes me unhappy, deeply unhappy."

"How can I apologize?" Masuto asked him. "My wife's family is more important than my own."

"Your wife's family is your family."

"Yes, and I am cursed with being a policeman, and time, which is so precious, is denied to me."

"Some of us have wondered about the life you chose."

"It is my karma."

"Don't talk to me of karma," Orashi said. "I am a Christian, as you know."

"A thousand apologies."

"I am being hard on you," Orashi said, "but I still have affection for you—even though I know that it is your work and not your own affection that brings you here."

"So, it is true. What can I say?"

"Nothing. I will tell you. You come here to talk about

the skeleton found under the swimming pool in Beverly Hills."

"Yes, but how—"

"Enough, Masao! I read the papers. I exist in the world. Who else will tell you anything about a house built thirty years ago?"

"Of course."

"Have you been to see Mrs. Brody? I believe she still lives on Maple Street in Inglewood, though I have not been to see her since Alex died. So I am as culpable as you, Masao. She is very lonely, I imagine."

"No. She's dead."

"Poor woman. When did she die?"

"She was murdered this morning."

"God rest her soul. You come with bad news, my nephew."

"I live with bad news."

"Yes, I suppose you do. Do you know who killed her?"

"I think I do, but who he is, I don't know."

"Is it a game, Masao? You know who killed her, but not who he is? You have been too long with the Zen people. They teach you to talk in riddles."

"Not at all, my respected uncle. We will talk about that. Meanwhile, I am glad that you knew Alex Brody. Perhaps it will help me."

"Thirty years ago I knew all the contractors in this area. I helped Brody. He was what the young people call a loser. He was one of those who never calculate a job properly, and in their eagerness for the contract, they underbid. Up until nineteen fifty both of us built only very small houses, bungalows, such as the one he lived in in Inglewood. He wanted desperately to move into a more profitable area, and he bid on the house on Laurel Way. I told him his bid was too low, that prices were going up, and that the hillside would present difficulties. In nineteen forty-seven he had worked for me on a job, and that was how we became acquainted. He respected my ability to calculate, and he would bring me bids to look over. I did it as a favor. He was a kind man, not too intelligent, but kind, and I liked him. He knew his bid was too low, but he felt that he could cut corners. He was too honest to cut corners, and he came out of the job eight thousand dollars in debt. Real dollars, not the ones we have today. He never recovered from that loss, poor man, and ten years later he died of a heart attack."

"But he did complete the house on Laurel Way?"

"Certainly. And a very good job too."

"And he put in the swimming pool?"

"Yes, and that was a mistake. He had never built a pool before, and his calculations were way off. He had to buttress the hillside, and that was where he took his loss."

"May I explain my previous statement that you found confusing?" Masuto asked him.

With a twinkle in his eye, Naga suggested that perhaps they should speak in Japanese. "A difficult language, but not confusing. English is even more difficult and totally confusing."

"My Japanese is confusing, believe me. It confuses both myself and the listener. What I meant before, when I said that I knew who killed Mrs. Brody, was that I am quite certain I can connect him with the other murder."

"What other murder?" Naga asked innocently.

"The body placed under the swimming pool. I am

quite certain, in my own mind, that the same person who put the body there murdered Mrs. Brody."

"Ah, so," Naga agreed. "And now you come to this poor old Japanese gentleman and you wish me to remember who was on Alex Brody's crew when he built the swimming pool, and when I tell you that, you will sort out the various people and you will have the murderer."

"Exactly."

"And this, Masao, is how you built your reputation for brilliance in the field of crime?"

He disliked being teased, even by Kati's uncle, whose years earned him that prerogative. "If I had such a reputation, it is undeserved. I poke around in the dark. I chase ghosts. And I hope for luck."

"Nephew, how could I possibly know who worked for Alex? It was thirty years ago. For a swimming pool, you need backhoe men, pick and shovel laborers, masons. Was the swimming pool dug in dirt or in decayed granite?"

"Decayed granite."

"And a groove was made for the body?"

"Precisely."

"Then you have two possibilities, Masao. If the killer was strong and energetic, he could have come back to the job after the crew had left for the day, and by working very hard with a pickax and crowbar, he could have dug the grave in the decayed granite. It varies, you know."

Masao shook his head. "I didn't know."

"Oh, yes. Sometimes it is so hard it must be blasted out. At other times it is as soft as gravel. How large was the hole where you found the remains?"

"About six feet long, two feet wide, a foot deep."

"Ah, so. And when he finished, I imagine he packed the soft granite back into the hole, and then when the swimming pool slid down the hillside, the rain washed out enough fill to reveal the skeleton. You think he used a backhoe?"

"Yes."

"Wrong, Masao. Shall I explain why? Over there." He pointed to where a group of caterpillar-tread machines were parked across the yard. "Those with the long necks, like geese, those are backhoes."

"I know what a backhoe is."

"But do you know how a backhoe works? You describe a grave about six feet long."

"Perhaps a few inches more," Masuto said.

"Now, the ends of the grave. They were perpendicular, like the end of a coffin?"

"More or less."

"Then we must ask, where did the scoop enter? It is not like a hand-held tool. That scoop must come down and dig its approach. It can't make the kind of a hole you describe. Now, nephew, let us have a few words on the construction of a swimming pool. The backhoe scoops it out. But if the backhoe scoops out the entire pool, how does the backhoe get out of the hole?"

"That never occurred to me," Masuto confessed. "I have never built a swimming pool."

"A humble man wins my heart. I will explain. Only a part of the hole is dug with the backhoe inside. Then the backhoe moves out of the pool and completes the excavation from above. We can do that because the scoop has a long neck which rides up and down the main hoist. In effect, the backhoe leans over the edge of the pool and scoops it out. The final shaping is done by laborers with pick and shovel, working inside the pool. Now, your murderer plans to dig a grave and bury his victim. He must wait until the backhoe is out of the pool and the laborers are finished and the concrete is ready to be poured. Otherwise how can he be sure his work will not be discovered? So we must presume that he dug the hole with a pickax shortly before the concrete was poured, that he was a laborer and not a backhoe operator. In fact, since backhoe rentals are expensive, and since Alex Brody did not own one, by the time he dug the grave, the backhoe was gone from the scene."

Fascinated by the old man's line of reasoning, Masuto listened and nodded.

"You disagree?"

"Oh, no, not at all. I am everlastingly grateful. And now, if you will tell me where I can find this laborer, I shall be even more grateful."

"After thirty years? No, for that you must go to one of your Zen magicians."

"Zen masters are not magicians," Masuto said gently. "Just people. Surely there must be some lead, some way of discovering who worked for Alex Brody."

"Have you looked for his records? His payroll records?"

"If any survived, the murderer found them and took them."

"In any case, the killer's name would not be his real name," Naga said. "He would have been very foolish to use his real name."

"I am not looking for his name. I want the name of the man he killed."

"Oh? You puzzle me, nephew."

"Wasn't there a foreman on that job?"

"There would be, yes."

"Can you remember? Try."

The old man knit his brows. "As much as I would like to help you, my dear nephew—it was so long ago. He once used Jim Adams, who came to work for me later, but Adams died two years ago. Ah, wait—Fred—Fred Lundman. I'm pretty sure he was on that job. Fred was a good man. He went out on his own after that, and he did very well building tract houses in the Valley. Yes, I do think he worked with Alex up there on Laurel Way."

"Is he still alive?" Masuto asked excitedly.

"I think so."

"Do you know where he lives?"

"Last I heard, he had built himself a fine house in Brentwood."

"Uncle Naga, do you have a telephone? But of course you do!"

"Ah, yes. We have all the modern conveniences. Come with me."

Containing an impulse to beg the old man to hurry, Masuto followed him across the yard to the main office. "You will use my office, and I will prepare some tea. Your aunt still makes the best tea cakes I know of, and we have been entirely too unceremonious. It is not fitting."

Masuto found the number in the telephone book, Frederick Lundman, on the Bristol Circles in Brentwood, a very pleasant part of Los Angeles which lies between Westwood and Santa Monica. He dialed the number and heard it ring. It rang again and again; it rang ten times before Masuto put down the telephone and whispered, "What a fool—what an incredible fool I am!"

He dialed again, this time calling Los Angeles police headquarters, and this time the phone was answered. Masuto asked for Pete Bones. When he heard Bones's voice, Masuto said, "Here's an address. I want a prowl car there, quickly please."

"Why?"

"Damn it, Pete! Will you listen to me for once." He gave him the address. "I'm over on the east edge of Whittier. I'll go straight there, but it takes time."

"Goddamnit, Masuto, you can't push us around that way. What's going on?"

"I don't know," Masuto said tiredly, convinced suddenly that it was too late, that this part of it was over. "I just don't know." He put down the telephone and turned to face his uncle.

"I see that we will not have tea," Naga said. "I have been making light of something that is terrible."

Masuto nodded.

"We inhabit an unhappy universe, Masuto. What has happened?"

"I don't know. Perhaps nothing."

"You think that Fred Lundman is dead."

"I hope not. I must make one more call."

"Please."

He dialed the number of the police station in Beverly Hills and asked for Beckman.

"I got nothing," Beckman said. "This John Doe of ours stepped out of nowhere and laid down under the swimming pool and died. That's where we are and that's what it adds up to. And you want to know about bronze stars and oakleaf clusters and purple hearts, the army can lend us maybe two, three thousand names, providing you want to make a trip to the Pentagon and go through their records. So I got another notion, schools that teach kung fu and jujitsu and that stuff you specialize in—?"

"Karate."

"Right, karate. So I did a little rundown just here in L.A., and we got over four hundred places—"

"Forget it, Sy. Forget the whole thing. I want you to meet me in Brentwood. You'll get there first. It's the home of a Mr. Fred Lundman, and if everything's cool there, just hang in until I arrive. But in any case, wait there for me." He gave Beckman the address.

"You will come again on a happier occasion, with Kati and the children?" Naga asked.

"I'll come again, yes."

Driving to Brentwood from Naga's place, a disturbing thought nagged at Masuto. He had seen the toothmarks of a backhoe at the edge of the grave. Then why had Naga tried so hard to convince him that the grave had not been dug by a backhoe? Or had he been mistaken in believing that the marks had been made by a backhoe?

5

FRED LUNDMAN

Lieutenant Pete Bones was standing on the lawn in front of the big stucco house at the Bristol Circles, arguing loudly with Sy Beckman when Masuto drove up and parked his old Datsun behind an L.A.P.D. prowl car. On the other side of the prowl car an ambulance was backed into the driveway, and beyond that the medical examiner's car and Bones's car and then another police car. It was a quiet suburban neighborhood, very upper middle class and unused to such attention. A circle of housewives, maids, and children stood gaping and whispering.

When he saw Masuto, Bones broke off his exchange with Beckman and strode over to the Beverly Hills policeman, telling him angrily, "You got one hell of a lot of explaining to do, Masuto."

"I suppose so."

"What in hell does that mean—you suppose so? Do you know what happened in there?"

"I can guess," Masuto replied morosely.

"You can guess! You and your goddamn guesses! There are two people dead in there, and you knew damn well what was coming down. Do you know what that adds up to? It adds up to something that stinks!"

"Suppose we go inside and talk about it there."

"And more quietly," Beckman said. He was three inches taller than Bones and at least six inches wider. "Who the hell do you think you are, lacing us out like that? You got something to say, say it like a colleague, not like some crumbum hoodlum."

"Just who the hell do you think you are, Beckman? I don't take that crap from anyone!"

"Hold it, hold it," Masuto said soothingly. "Come on, let's not get all hot and angry. Pete's got a point, Sy, and it's my fault. I should have filled him in better, but I never thought it would happen like this. Not so quickly."

As they headed toward the door of the house, Bones said, "You knew this was going to happen. You knew a man and a woman were going to be killed—"

"A woman?"

"That's right. You knew it and you knew how they'd be killed and you didn't lift a finger to stop it. And if that doesn't stink, I don't know what does. I ought to read you your rights here on the spot."

"Don't be an idiot!" Beckman snapped.

"That's enough. Now you listen to me, Pete," Masuto said harshly, "this is hard enough on me without you bearing down." They were at the door now. "Hold on, before we go in there. I was afraid that something like this would happen. That's why I called you this morning. But I didn't know where or who, and the fact that I got Lundman's name and address was a streak of luck. The moment I did I called you and told you to get a radio car over here. We were too late. Yes, that stinks, but the cases where cops can prevent a crime are few and far between. You know that as well as I do. Now just let me find out what happened in here, and I'll fill you in on everything."

Bones stared at him for a moment, then swallowed and nodded. "Okay. But you fill me in—with everything."

He led them into the house. It was a well-made, well-furnished home, done in the Spanish colonial style, tile floors, good pictures on the white-painted walls. Unlike Alex Brody, Lundman had done well. In the living room there were two bodies, already on ambulance litters, two ambulance men, Lloyd Abramson, from the medical examiner's office, a uniformed cop, a fingerprint man, two other Los Angeles plainclothes investigators, and a Mexican woman in a maid's uniform who sat in a chair and sobbed.

Masuto went to the litters and stared at the two bodies. One was a woman in her middle fifties, an attractive mild-looking woman, her face tormented with a mixture of pain and surprise. "Her neck was broken," Abramson said, pointing to the livid bruise. "I can't imagine what kind of an instrument would leave a mark like that. Pete thinks he used his hand. A karate chop."

"What about that?" Bones asked Masuto. "Could he kill her like that, with a single karate chop?"

"Yes, he could."

"Could you?"

48

"Yes, I could."

"What the hell is this?" Beckman asked harshly. "You making jokes? Masuto was in Whittier."

"Just a joke."

"A lousy joke," Beckman said.

Masuto went to the other litter. Lundman was in his late sixties, a heavy-set man, white hair, pale blue eyes wide open. "Same thing," Abramson told him. "Neck broken. You'd think he'd put up a struggle. He's old, but he's built like a bull."

"Pull up his shirt," Masuto said to one of the ambulance men.

Bones was watching him curiously. "Go on, pull up his shirt," Bones said.

Masuto pointed to a bruise directly under the rib cage. "A hard blow to the solar plexus. If you know how to deliver it, the result is temporary paralysis. The victim doubles over. Turn the body, please," he said to the ambulance men. They turned the dead man over, and Masuto pointed to the mark on the back of his neck. "A hard vertical chop."

"You're telling me that one chop with the bare hand would kill a man of his size?"

"His size doesn't matter. The weapon is the side of the hand. A chop like that, properly delivered, would split a plank an inch thick. The first blow doubled Lundman over, paralyzed him, and put his neck in position for the second blow, which broke his neck and killed him."

"Just like that?"

"Yes, just like that." Masuto stared at Bones quizzically. "Are you going to ask me whether I could do it?"

"Could you?"

"Yes. I take it the woman was Lundman's wife?"

"Clara Lundman. Yeah. His wife."

"And the maid? Where was the maid?"

"Downstairs in the basement doing the wash. She never heard a thing. She was still down there when the cops came."

"On your call?"

"That's right."

"How long between the time she went down to the basement and the time she heard the cops?"

"About an hour and a half."

"That's a lot of wash," Beckman said.

"She says she had ironing to do."

"How long were they dead when you got here?" Masuto asked Abramson.

"Can they take the bodies away now?" he asked Bones, who nodded. "It's hard to say exactly," he told Masuto. "I got here after the cops, about a half hour later. Maybe two hours to the time I got here. A little more, a little less."

"She said she served them lunch," Beckman said. "Then she cleared up and did the dishes. It was about two o'clock, she thinks, when she went down to do the wash. I got here same time as the L.A. cops. That was just about three thirty."

"I still don't know what puts you and Masuto here at all, except for that weird tipoff. This is Los Angeles, not Beverly Hills. Sure I'm extending the courtesies—"

"You're all courtesy," Beckman remarked.

"—but there's a limit. You read me a scenario about a guy who walks in here, takes a look at the woman who opens the door for him, kills her with a karate chop, then kills her husband the same way, and then makes his exit without even touching—hey, Steve"—he called to one of the L.A. investigators—"give me those envelopes with the possessions. Yeah, without even touching this stuff. Take a look."

He emptied one envelope onto the coffee table. "Diamond ring. With the price of ice these days, it's got to be maybe sixty, seventy grand. Gold bracelet. Emerald brooch—right on the front of her dress where he couldn't miss it."

Masuto picked it up and examined it, a large emerald set in a nest of rubies. "About thirty thousand dollars," he concluded. "Wouldn't you say so, Sy?"

"Just about."

"And a Swiss watch." He emptied the other envelope. "Lundman's wallet. Four hundred and twelve dollars in cash. Another Swiss watch. Sapphire pinky ring. And six credit cards. That killer is one indifferent son of a bitch."

"Or very rich and very careful. He's not a thief, he's a murderer. He takes no chances."

"Suppose we talk about him."

"Can you give me a little more time, Pete?" He grinned at Bones. "As long as you're not reading me my rights and we're cooperating?"

"All right. I shot off my mouth too quick. It's a habit."

"I want to talk to the maid and poke around the house. And I'd like Sy to talk to some of the people outside."

"We covered that. They see no evil and hear no evil."

"Nothing?"

"Nothing to write home about. One woman saw a car pull away down the street. She thinks it was a black Mercedes. She thinks a man was driving. No plate num-

51

bers, but she *thinks* it was a California plate. Could she describe the man? No. That's it, in a town where they're maybe five thousand black Mercedes."

"Two-door or four-door?"

"She thinks four-door."

"I'd still like Sy to talk to her."

"Okay. And what do I do—sit around and wait for you?"

"It's five o'clock now," Masuto said. "If you can make it at the Beverly Hills police station at seven, I'll give you all I have. I know that takes you out of your way, but Wainwright will be sore as hell if I spell it out for you and he doesn't know what's going on. Which he doesn't. Also, I haven't eaten all day."

"You're stretching it."

"I know."

"You got any more killings lined up for me?"

"I hope not."

"Okay. Wainwright's office at seven." He turned to Beckman. "Come on, I'll introduce you to our Mercedes witness."

The Lundman maid was full of grief and fear of the cold, unpredictable Anglo world that surrounded her. She spoke English, but Masuto felt that her own language would put her more at ease, and he asked her in Spanish what her name was.

"Rosita, señor."

"Good. We will speak in your tongue. You cared deeply for the Lundmans?"

"She was like a mother to me. Who would do this?"

"An evil man. You must not think of death now, only of your own life which was spared because you were downstairs. In this house, only Mr. and Mrs. Lundman lived?"

"Yes, señor. Only the two."

"Did they have children?"

"One son in San Francisco. He is an architect. I gave the police his telephone number and they called him. He was close to them. He will feel great sorrow." She began to sob again, and Masuto waited.

"When you were downstairs, the door to the basement was closed?"

"Yes, señor."

"Were any of the machines going? I mean the washing machine."

"Yes, the dryer. I was ironing Mr. Lundman's shirts, and the towels were in the dryer."

"The man who came, he must have rung the doorbell. Did you hear it?"

"No, señor. In the basement, when the door is closed, you don't hear the doorbell. When I work down there, I leave the door open."

"Why did you close it this time?"

"Mrs. Lundman asked me to. She said she would get the door if anyone came."

"Was she expecting someone?"

"I don't know, señor."

"But when the police came, they rang the bell and you heard it. How was that? Had the clothes dryer stopped?"

She looked at him bewilderedly. "Yes, it stopped."

"But you said that even without the dryer going, when the door is closed, you don't hear the bell."

"Señor," she whispered, "the door to the basement was open."

Masuto stood up. "Come, Rosita, we're going down to the basement."

"Please, señor, not now. I am afraid."

"It will be all right, Rosita. Just stay behind me." He drew his revolver, and the remaining L.A. investigator, still in the living room, said, "What's that for?"

"I'm not sure," Masuto told him. "The killer opened the basement door. It's a million-to-one shot against him still being there, but why take chances?"

"We looked in the basement."

"We'll look again. Is there an outside door to the basement?" he asked Rosita.

"Yes, there is."

The door leading to the basement was in the kitchen, and the staircase was dark. Masuto flicked on the light. "Do you leave this light on when you work in the basement?"

"No, there is a switch at the bottom of the staircase. There are windows in the laundry room."

"He didn't leave by the basement," the L.A. investigator said. "The basement door has a dead bolt and it was locked from the inside."

They went down the stairs and searched the basement. There was a short corridor at the foot of the basement stairs. To the left was a room that contained the furnace and the hot water heater. The laundry room was to the right, and opening off the laundry room, Rosita's room. Both rooms had high, narrow windows.

"You turned off the dryer," Masuto said to Rosita. "What did you do then?"

"I was tired, señor. I went into my room and closed the door and lay down on my bed and smoked a ciga-rette."

Masuto noticed an ashtray with a cigarette butt in it. "Then if he had looked in the cellar, he would not have seen you—unless he went into your room?"

"Oh, my God."

"I was beginning to believe he made no mistakes."

"How's that?" the L.A. investigator asked.

"Maybe one mistake. I want to go through the house with Rosita."

"The lieutenant said to give you your head."

Masuto looked at Rosita. "How old are you, Rosita?"

"Twenty-three." She was very simply, plainly beautiful, and it occurred to Masuto that when Mexican or Japanese women are beautiful, they have a kind of beauty that no Western European woman can match, a kind of earthy openness that harks back to the beginning of things.

"You are very young, and you have a long life ahead of you. We must see that you come to no harm."

"I am so afraid."

"Now you are with me, Rosita, and there is nothing to be afraid of. I promise you that. Now we will go upstairs."

The L.A. investigator was listening to them. "She speaks English," he said with some annoyance. "You got something I shouldn't hear?"

"She's more comfortable in her language, just as I imagine you are more comfortable in yours."

"They come here and go on welfare; you'd think they'd learn to talk the damn language."

"It was their country. We came here," Masuto said gently, taking the girl's arm and leading her up the stairs.

"What the hell is that supposed to mean?"

He led her from room to room, two bedrooms, a den

with a television set in it. "Look at everything, Rosita. Tell me if anything's been touched or moved."

In the bedrooms nothing had been touched. In the master bedroom, there was a jewel box on the dressing table. Evidently, the Lundmans did not believe in locking away their valuables in a safe deposit box. Masuto raised the lid and stared at the array of pearls, diamonds, and gold chains.

"She always kept them here, Rosita, like this?"

"She said they were insured, and that if she couldn't enjoy them, there was no use having them."

"She trusted you."

"Yes, señor." The tears began again.

In the den there was a large mahogany desk. It contained a file drawer. "That was opened," Rosita said.

"How do you know?"

"You see, it is not closed completely. I am careful. I keep the drawers closed."

Masuto opened the file drawer and glanced through it. "Mr. Lundman was retired?"

"Yes. Last year he retired."

Evidently, he had kept ten years of business and personal financial records. Even if his records had gone back thirty years, as the foreman on the job he would keep no records of workers. The killer must have known that. He had opened the file out of curiosity. As Masuto had already surmised, he was a curious and methodical man. He would give himself a specific length of time in the house, perhaps ten minutes, which he would consider a safe interval. He would check the house, check the basement.

Masuto shook his head in exasperation. I am working from the wrong end, he told himself. I am following him. He's too smart for that. The only way is to begin at the beginning, but what is the beginning and why?

"Do you have a family?" he asked Rosita.

"In Mexico City, señor."

"No one here? No dear friend?"

"I am only here three years, señor, and all the time working here for the Lundmans."

"No man you love and can trust?"

"Oh, señor!"

"Then you must trust me, Rosita. I'm going to take you with me. I'm not going to arrest you, but you must not stay here. You see, the newspapers and television people, who are outside by now, well, they will report that you were here when the murders took place. You didn't see the murderer, but there is no way that he can be sure of that. And that means that he will come after you."

"Dear Mother of God, señor, what will I do?"

"You will not be afraid. You will come with me and you will do what I tell you to do. Is that clear?"

"Yes—but the house?"

"The house will be sealed and an officer will remain here until Mr. Lundman's son comes. We'll go downstairs, and you will go to your room and change into a plain dress. Pack a small bag, a change of clothes, toothbrush, things of that sort, enough for a few days. Then wait for me in your room."

They went downstairs, and as Rosita started for the basement door, the L.A. investigator demanded to know where she was going.

"To her room for the moment. I'm taking her with me."

Beckman entered as the L.A. man shouted, "What the

hell do you mean, you're taking her with you! The lieutenant says she stays here."

"For Christ's sake, Billy," Beckman said, "what's with you guys? We're on your side. If Masuto says he's taking her, he's got a damn good reason."

"I'm meeting Pete Bones at seven," Masuto said soothingly. "When I see him, I'll have the girl with me. But meanwhile, I want to remind you that she's not under arrest. She can't be detained. She has the right to come and go as she pleases, and in a few minutes we're going out through the back basement door, which you can lock behind us."

"You're building one big pile of trouble for yourself, sergeant."

"We'll try to live with it."

Downstairs, Rosita was ready and waiting, and as they went out through the cellar door, Beckman said, "They are one lovely bunch, those L.A. cops. Just sweet, kind, gentle souls."

"They do their job."

"So do we. There are ways."

6
ROSITA

They stopped to eat at a Mexican restaurant in Westwood, halfway between Brentwood and Beverly Hills. Once a small, pretty college town, Westwood was now a contiguous part of Los Angeles, although still dominated by UCLA. The little restaurant was packed with students. Rosita watched them wistfully. "They seem so alive and happy," she said in Spanish. "It's hard to understand being happy."

"Give it time," Masuto said. "We'll speak English. My friend, Detective Beckman, has trouble with Spanish."

His mouth full of tamales and beans, Beckman was having no trouble with Mexican food. He finished chewing and said, "Four years of high school Spanish—it's the way they teach, Masao, lousy. My wife says I should take a course in night school. Then I'd never see her. Maybe she's right. Anyway, we got nothing from that dame who saw the Mercedes. Now she says maybe it was a Jaguar. But I found a kid who says it was a black Mercedes, a four-fifty SL. The kid is a mavin on cars, so what he saw is dependable, but he didn't look at the plates or who was driving."

"The four-fifty is a two-door sports car. Bones said the woman saw a four-door. It's like confusing a grapefruit with a tangerine."

"That occurred to me. So maybe we got nothing."

"Which is what we had to begin with—a corpse that doesn't exist and a killer who doesn't exist."

"Except that according to you, the corpse is the killer. Bones will love that."

"I don't think Bones loves anything, not even himself. Wait for me outside the station, Sy, and then I want you to take Rosita here into our office and stay with her. Also, call Kati and tell her I'll be late."

"What do I tell my wife?"

"Tell her you've started night school in Spanish."

Rosita smiled. It was the first time Masuto had seen her smile. She was even prettier when she smiled.

When Masuto walked into Wainwright's office at the Beverly Hills police station, three men were waiting for him along with Wainwright. There was Pete Bones and with him his boss, Captain Kennedy of the L.A. police, whom Masuto had tangled with before, and a short, hard-faced man who was introduced as Chief Morrison of the Inglewood police. On Wainwright's face was a look of pained yet resigned sufferance, an expression Masuto was not unfamiliar with. "Sit down, Masao," he said bleakly.

"I'm here in Beverly Hills when I should be at home,"
Kennedy said, "because, goddamnit, you're pulling one
of your stunts again, Masuto, and so help me God, this
time you're going to give us the bottom line. The lieutenant here says he was ready to read you your rights,
and maybe he went too far, but first you're down in
Inglewood on a murder nobody knows about yet, and
then you call Bones and tell him today is killing day and
then you turn up before the bodies are cold—and just
what in the hell is this all about? You people turn up a
skeleton that was put under a swimming pool thirty
years ago, and now we got a slaughterhouse all over
L.A. County."

"It appears that way, doesn't it," Masuto agreed.

"What do you mean, appears?" Morrison snapped.
"You're a Beverly Hills cop. You think something's
going on in Inglewood, you call me. You don't go barg-
ing down to our turf like you got a license for the whole
county. Maybe that old lady would still be alive if you
had followed proper procedure."

"Would she?" Masuto asked mildly. "Or would you
tell me that no crime has been committed and that there
was nothing you could do? Or would you tell me that
since she hadn't testified or agreed to testify at a pre-trial
hearing, the rules didn't permit you to give her protection. I wasn't born yesterday, hardly, and I've been a cop
for a long time. So if you're ready to listen to me and
hear what I have, I'll spell it out for you. Otherwise,
forget it. My boss is Captain Wainwright here. I don't
owe the rest of you one damn thing."

"For Christ's sake, Masao," Wainwright exclaimed,
"we're cooperating! We're not like the army and navy.
We're all on the same side."

"Cool down," Kennedy said. "Maybe we're too hard on you. But if you let us in on things along the way, it would be easier."

"He don't even let me in," Wainwright said. "He's the Lone Ranger. The trouble is he's good. He's the best damn plainclothes cop this city ever had. So why don't we listen to him?"

"Go ahead," Kennedy said.

"All right," Masuto agreed. "Saturday it rained, on top of a winter of too much rain. A swimming pool on Laurel Way slid down into the canyon, and we found this skeleton under it. We pegged it as put there thirty years ago, and my partner, Sy Beckman, put in some work yesterday and got dates and the name of the builder out of the town records. I made some guesses. One: the killer worked in the excavation. Two: the victim worked in the excavation. I have reasons for my guesses, but I won't go into them now. Anyway, thirty years go by. You don't have to be a genius to decide that the first person to see is the building contractor, providing he's still alive. Let me underline something. It was *our* killing, a Beverly Hills homicide. Alex Brody was the contractor. I had his address and I drove down to Inglewood, but I was too late. Not for Brody. He died years ago, but too late to save his wife, who may or may not have known something. The killer took no chances. He read about the pool in the newspapers or saw it on TV, and he decided to kill Mrs. Brody. If there was anything in her house to incriminate him, he took it with him. Then I called Pete here and asked about any homicide with a similar M.O. Then I drove to Whittier, where I have an uncle in the home-building business.

He's an old man, and he knows everyone who operates in L.A. County. He remembered that Lundman was the foreman on that Laurel Way job, and as soon as I heard that, I called Bones and I called my partner, Sy Beckman. I was too late. Do you think I enjoy living with that? But if you can tell me where I acted improperly, I'm ready to listen."

They were silent for a while after Masuto had finished. Then Kennedy said, "You tie it all together? You're convinced that the same man who killed the body under the pool did the killings today?"

"It's too tight to be a coincidence."

"Why now?"

"Because as long as his victim was safely under the pool, he had nothing to worry about."

"Suppose Brody and Lundman were alive? What could they give us? They didn't witness the murder. Why kill them?"

"They could give us the name of the man who was killed."

"Come on, Masuto. So you got a name for the victim," Bones said. "What does that change?"

"Everything. Because my guess is that the killer took his victim's name and identity. Once you have the victim's identity, you can find the murderer in the telephone book."

"What do you base that on?" Wainwright wanted to know.

"Bits and pieces. The body was put in the grave naked. The reaction of the killer today. What Kennedy here said. Why kill people who weren't witnesses? The mind, the ego, the personality of the killer."

63

"What in hell do you know about his personality?" Morrison asked. He had listened scowling, looking uncomfortable at being lectured to by an Oriental.

"A good deal. He's pathological, without conscience, indifferent to any usual standards of right and wrong. He's highly intelligent in terms of being able to plan and calculate precisely. He's careful. He leaves no loose ends. He's five feet eight or nine inches in height, muscular, well built, in excellent physical condition. He exercises regularly. He's well off, possibly wealthy, compulsively neat—"

"Bullshit!" Morrison exclaimed.

"As you wish."

The others began to laugh. Still not mollified, Morrison said, "You got a murder thirty years ago, and you tell me the killer's walking around knocking off people with his bare hands. That's a hard pill to swallow. You tell our cops that he killed the old lady with brass knucks, and now it's changed to a bare hands job."

"He analyzes. When he makes a mistake, he moves immediately to correct it. The brass knucks was an error. It involves a weapon, and a weapon is incriminating. He got rid of the brass knuckles."

"And kills with his bare hands? One blow? I don't buy that crap."

"I can split a brick with one blow of my bare hand," Masuto said quietly, watching Morrison.

"Maybe we should consider that."

"Morrison," Kennedy said, "will you lay off that tack. We asked for an explanation and the sergeant's given us one." He turned to Masuto. "If all we need to turn up this bastard is the name of the man he killed, providing you're guessing right, there are ways. Someone must have put out a missing report or some kind of inquiry?"

"I don't think so. A lot of laborers are drifters, no home, no family. They pick up jobs here and there, unskilled work, pick and shovel work, fruit picking, that kind of thing. We have no fingerprints and no dental work. The man never had a cavity filled. Beckman spent most of yesterday trying to get a lead that way. Nothing."

"The F.B.I.?"

"Nothing."

"Could we go back to that Laurel Way job? Maybe someone besides the contractor and the foreman?"

Masuto shrugged. "Thirty years. We can try. But the killer's a lot more familiar with that job than we are, and if there are any leads in that direction, he'll get rid of them. Was there another murder today?"

"Not that we know of."

"Then I suspect he's closed the doors."

"What about the black Mercedes?" Bones asked.

"Beckman found a kid who says it was a two-door four-fifty SL."

"So much for that."

"Fingerprints?" Kennedy asked.

"This man wouldn't leave prints."

"Then we got nothing. Not one damn lousy thing."

"We have something," Masuto said. "The Lundmans' maid, Rosita, was in the basement of the house when it happened. The killer made a quick tour of the house, but he missed her. That's his only mistake to date."

"What kind of mistake?" Bones demanded. "She didn't see him."

"But he doesn't know that. The media's told the world that she was there."

"The media's also told the world that she didn't see him."

"He can't depend on that," Masuto said. "That could be a ploy to put him off his guard. He has to get rid of her. He's not a man who takes chances or depends on luck."

"Where is she now?" Kennedy asked.

"She's in my office with Beckman."

"I told her to stay in the house," Bones said.

"Yes. I asked her to come with me. She agreed."

"What in hell do you mean, she agreed? Where do you come off countermanding my orders in an L.A. jurisdiction? There was a cop in the house. I wanted her there."

"Just cool down," Masuto said, his annoyance beginning to show. "She wasn't under arrest. She can go where she damn pleases. I decided she wasn't safe in that house, and she agreed and went with me."

"With a cop there?"

"Yes, with a cop there."

"All right," Kennedy said. "You two can stop scrapping. She's here. What now?"

"I want you to give her key witness protection, to put her up in some hotel with guards in constant attendance."

"She's not a key witness."

"It comes to the same thing. Her life is in danger."

"So you say, Masuto. The way I look at it, you're pulling this whole scenario out of your hat. Maybe you're right and maybe you're wrong. But you know we can't treat her as a key witness. She isn't a witness. She can't testify to anything, and we can't bend the rules and spend a bundle of city money because you got intuition. She's free to go back to the house, where there'll be a cop on guard for the next twenty-four hours. That's all we can do."

"There's something else you can do."

"What's that?"

"You can pay the burial expenses when she's killed. She has no family here."

"You got a big mouth, Masuto. It's going to buy you a lot of trouble some day."

When they had gone and Masuto was alone with Wainwright, the captain said to him, "Kennedy's right, Masao. The last people in the world we need as enemies are the L.A. cops. You know that. We depend on them for a lot of things, not to mention those fancy computers they got down there. We're a small city with a small police force. All right, we got a thirty-year-old murder up there on Laurel Way. The city manager isn't breathing down my neck, and the mayor says the best thing we can do, since it's nobody anybody ever heard about, is to let the hullabaloo die down and close the file."

"You're not serious?"

"I'm serious, Masao."

"This lunatic has killed three people today, and you're telling me to close the file?"

"It's not our jurisdiction. The headache belongs to Inglewood and to Los Angeles, and we got enough headaches of our own. Anyway, this lunatic, as you call him, only connects with Laurel Way on your say-so."

"Captain, you don't believe that."

"I believe what the city manager tells me to believe. Yesterday he was on my back. Today he's off my back."

"You said you'd give me until Wednesday, and if I turned up something then, you'd give me the rest of the week. I think I've turned up a good deal."

"I said if you turned up the name of the deceased. That's what counts. Find me a movie star or a hotshot businessman under the pool, and I'll give you your head. But John Doe without even a name tag just doesn't rate it."

"But I have until Wednesday?"

"I said so, didn't I?"

"And what about the girl, Rosita?" Masuto asked gently.

"What about her?"

"She has to be put in a hotel room with protection."

"Come on, Masao, you heard what Kennedy said. Like I said, this is out of our jurisdiction. We got no obligation to this girl."

"We have an obligation to keep a human being alive. What will it cost, a few hundred dollars and a few days of time for an officer?"

"You can take her back to Brentwood. They got a cop there."

"And make her a sitting duck. No, thank you."

"Masao, I'm not made of stone, but there's no way I can justify this, no way."

Masuto went back to his office, where Rosita was carefully improving Beckman's bad Spanish. *"A qué se dedica usted?"*

"Got it. I'm a cop, right?"

"Right," Rosita said.

"How did it go?" Beckman asked Masuto.

"As it always goes, like trying to swim in a pool of molasses."

"Are they off your back?"

"For the time being."

"And what do we do with the kid?"

"What would your wife say if you pulled duty for tonight?"

"You got to ask?" He nodded at Rosita. "Is that what you have in mind? I'll tell you what she'd say. She'd say she isn't too old to divorce me."

"Then you'd better lie." He pointed to the telephone. "Now?"

"Do it now, Sy. But let me specify that this is outside the line of duty. I can't force you."

"She's a sweet kid. If I was ten years younger—ah, what the hell!"

He called his wife, and while he made his excuses, Masuto said to Rosita, "I'm going to take you to a hotel, and Detective Beckman here will stay with you. I'm doing this because I feel you are in great danger. Hopefully, it will only be for a few days. But Mr. Beckman is a good, decent man and there's nobody in the world I trust more."

"If you say this, I believe you."

"Which is more than my wife does," Beckman said. "Where are we going, Masao?"

"To the Beverly Glen Hotel."

"You got to be kidding. That's the most expensive place in town. Wainwright would never spring for it."

"I know that. We'll give it a try anyhow. It's the last place our karate expert would look for her. Eventually he'll find her. But it gives us time. Now listen, Sy. I'll go first, with her in the car. Give me a block or so, and then follow me. If you pick up a car following us and you're sure it's a tail, cut it off and don't hesitate to use your gun. I know you can take care of yourself but this one is something else. Don't give him a chance to get close to you and don't try to put cuffs on him."

"You're thinking of the black Mercedes?"

"He could change cars—no, I'm just reacting to this insane world we inhabit. He couldn't know about Rosita until he heard the six o'clock news, and maybe they didn't have it there. It's a thousand to one shot, but I don't even want those odds."

No one followed Masuto, and Beckman pulled up at the Beverly Glen Hotel a minute or so after Masuto arrived. The Beverly Glen, a large, rambling pile of pink stucco, was almost as famous as Beverly Hills, a watering place for New York agents, actors, international jet-set characters, business tycoons, Mafia chiefs, high-priced call girls, and rich tourists who wished to rub shoulders with the general assortment of boarders. The hotel was managed by Al Gellman, a harassed, balding man in his mid-forties, who in any given month encountered everything imaginable excepting a major earthquake.

Now, in his office, he shook hands with Masuto and looked dubiously at Beckman and Rosita. "What is it, sergeant?" he asked. "We've had a quiet day so far, no drunks beating up on women, no fights at the bar, no one trying to stiff us on a room—but the day isn't over, is it?"

"I need a favor, Al," Masuto said.

"Whatever I can do. I owe you."

"I want to put this lady in a room with Beckman here to guard her, and I want it very quiet."

"You're bringing me trouble, sergeant."

"No. No one knows she's here and no one will know."

"It will cost. The best I can do with two adjoining rooms is two hundred and twenty a day."

"You said you owed me, Al. The city won't pay for this. I want three days free."

"Free!"

"With meals."

"I can't do it. It's out of the question. There's no way I can justify it."

"You find a way, Al. We've helped you out of more rough spots than you can shake a stick at. I've bent the law a dozen times. You've parked a hundred cars illegally on the streets around here, not once, but maybe two hundred times. We've never shaken you down, not for a nickel. Suppose we were to tell you the streets were off limits for parking? How many weddings would you cater then, how many balls? All I'm asking is a humanitarian gesture that won't cost you a cent. This is off season for you. You've got the space."

"If this is straight, why won't the city pay?"

"Because it's out of Beverly Hills jurisdiction. I'm not trying to con you. I'm trying to save this kid's life."

Gellman was silent for a long moment, and then he asked, "Can this be kept among us? I can't put it on the books and I can't let them register—which means I'm breaking the law."

"Let's say bending it a little. I don't want them on the register. Feed them sandwiches and coffee. They can survive on that for three days. Beckman will pick it up in the kitchen. And as far as we're concerned, no one will know."

"How about Wainwright?"

"He doesn't know and he won't know."

"Aren't you going out on a limb, sergeant?"

"I don't think so. We're breaking no law. There's no failure to register with intent to defraud or commit a crime. We're taking normal security precautions with a witness to a crime, and if the owners should come down on you, I give you my word I'll pay up myself. It won't be easy, but it won't break me."

Rosita, who had been listening intently, now said to Masuto in Spanish, "I have eleven hundred dollars in the bank I can pay."

"You'll need that money."

"My Spanish is as good as yours, sergeant," Gellman said, smiling. "I'll give you the three days. What the hell, it's a cold, hard world out there. I got a kid of my own her age."

7

DR. LEO
HARTMAN

It was after nine o'clock when Masuto finally parked his car in front of his house in Culver City. Ever since Kati had joined a consciousness-raising group of Nisei women —with his encouragement—Masuto had been uneasy when a case kept him to late hours. There were days when he regretted his liberal stance on the question of women's rights. He had married a lovely woman who, while born in California, had been raised in the old-fashioned Japanese manner, and it was with a sense of unease that he watched the changes taking place in her character. Tonight, he expected at least some degree of annoyance from Kati. Instead, he was surprised and pleased when she greeted him with a kiss and a pleasant smile.

He undressed and lay for a few minutes in a steaming hot bath, deciding during that interval that he would make no mention of the fact that he had filled his stomach with tamales and brown beans. Even through the closed bathroom door he could hear the sizzle of tempura and faintly smell the delicate shrimp, the green beans, and the sweet potato, all of it fried to fawn-colored perfection. Kati's opinion of Mexican food would have been unprintable, had Kati been given to saying unprintable things, and Masao also knew that she had delayed her own dinner, feeding the children and putting them to bed, so that she might share her evening meal with her husband. While he could not account for this defection from the rights of modern woman, he was in no way disposed to condemn it.

Clad in a black robe, his bare feet in comfortable sandals, he sat across the table from his wife and managed to deal adequately with the tempura. But he could not refrain from asking for some explanation of her behavior.

"Oh, I did consider being very provoked at your coming home at such an hour, but then I thought of how sweet and patient you have been for the past week, locked up in the house while the rain poured down, and never complaining while your vacation was completely spoiled. So I decided that a man with your qualities deserves tender loving care—unless of course this becomes a habit with you."

"God forbid."

"Also, my Uncle Naga telephoned and told me you had been to visit him, and he was very impressed with the respect you showed him. He feels that in this barbarian society respect for an old man is most commendable."

"Your Uncle Naga never approved of our marriage.

I don't think he ever forgave you for marrying a police-man."

"That's nonsense. He gave us a set of sterling silver dinnerware. I think that's very approving."

"Or a suggestion that I could never afford such a set myself."

"That is silly. Anyway, he told me that the skeleton on Laurel Way has turned into something horrible."

"Yes, it has. Your uncle talks too much."

"Uncle Naga is very clever. He said that from what you told him, you felt that the murderer had killed the man whose skeleton was found in order to steal his identity. Then the murderer could become someone else."

"Yes, more or less."

"But why should the murderer have to become some-one else?"

"I don't know. I've never had a case like this, Kati. There is absolutely nothing to go on. A man was killed thirty years ago, and there appears to be no way in the world to find out who he was. I'm convinced we'll never find out who he was."

"But isn't it more important to find the man who killed him? If he took the dead man's identity, then you will know who the dead man was."

"You make it sound very simple."

"If he wanted a new identity, he must have done something terrible. He had to hide."

"No doubt," Masuto agreed.

"But what good would all this trouble and evil he went to do, if he could still be recognized?"

Masuto stopped eating and stared at her.

"Why are you looking at me that way, Masao?"

"Go on. Don't stop. What were you saying?"

"I mean that if a man does something truly terrible and he has to kill someone to find a new identity, then wouldn't the police everywhere be looking for him? Wouldn't his picture be in the papers?"

"Yes, of course," Masuto said softly. "There are really no limits to my own stupidity. Then tell me, Kati, what would he do in such circumstances?"

"He could go to Europe or Brazil. I read that such people go to Brazil."

"No, he is here."

"Why does he stay here?"

"I don't know. Apparently, that was his plan from the beginning—to remain here."

"Then, Masao, I think he would go to a plastic surgeon and have his face changed."

"Yes, he would, wouldn't he," Masuto said slowly. "I know why I continue to be a policeman. It is because I lack the intelligence to be anything else. A plastic surgeon. He could have left the country, but apparently he didn't want to."

"Could such a man be in love with a woman?"

"Yes, but how could he explain plastic surgery to a woman?"

"Tell her he was in a bad accident, an auto crash?"

"Possibly. On the other hand, he may have determined to remain here simply because this is where he wanted to be. If it was plastic surgery, then there must be some record of it. On the other hand, knowing how he works—"

"Why don't you see Dr. Leo Hartman?"

"Who is Dr. Leo Hartman?"

"The most important plastic surgeon in Beverly Hills."

Once again Masuto stopped eating to stare at Kati. "How do you know such things?"

"I read newspapers and magazines, Masao. You can go everywhere. I must stay here with the children, so I read."

As early as Masuto might arise, Kati was always awake first, and this morning, when he entered the kitchen at seven o'clock, his pot of tea and his bowl of rice was ready. Since he was already dressed in his working clothes, gray flannels and a tweed jacket, Kati expressed surprise at the fact that he apparently did not intend to meditate.

"I thought I would drive down to the Zendo," Masuto explained. "I have not been there in quite a while, and I feel a need to talk to the Roshi."

"Can he solve crimes?" Kati asked lightly.

"Only the crimes honest people commit."

"Why, whenever I ask a question that relates to Zen, must you give me an answer that makes no sense?"

"Perhaps because Zen makes no sense."

"Do you see? That is exactly what I mean."

Masuto drove downtown thinking that his wife was a remarkable woman, whom he knew very little. Well, when it is so hard to know ourselves, why should we expect to know another?

The Zendo was a cluster of old frame buildings on Normandie Avenue off Pico Boulevard. The members of the Zendo, young married people, most of them from southern California, had bought the buildings cheaply—

77

since they were in an old, run-down neighborhood—renovated them, connected the backyards, and turned the whole thing into a sort of communal settlement. One of the houses had been made into a meditation hall with two slightly raised platforms running the length of a polished floor, and stained glass windows at one end. It was done with loving care, a cool, contemplative place. A Japanese Zen master had been sent from Kyoto to guide them, and this Roshi—as a Zen teacher is called—had been with them now for eleven years.

Masuto was a frequent visitor to the Zendo, and this morning he entered the meditation hall, removed his shoes, and composed himself to meditate. The hall was open to any who wished to come there to meditate, but by now, at a quarter to eight, the regular meditation was finished, and only the Roshi still sat, cross-legged. Masuto took his place facing the old man, and for the next forty minutes, they both sat in silence. Then the Roshi rose, and Masuto also rose and bowed to him.

"To come here with a gun in your armpit," the Roshi said, shaking his head.

"It is a part of my way of life."

"You come here only when you are troubled, as if the answers to the evils you encounter could be found here." He spoke in Japanese, and Masuto had to listen intently to follow his thought.

"And are there answers here?"

"If you are here, yes."

"I don't understand."

"Of course not. You are a fool. Can a fool understand?"

"I try."

"You know what a koan is, Masao. A koan is a question to which there is no answer. So you meditate upon it and find the answer."

"Even when there is no answer?"

"Only when there is no answer. Would it be a koan otherwise?"

Driving back to the Beverly Hills police station on Rexford Drive, Masuto reflected on his brief conversation with the Roshi and admitted to himself that he had derived little sustenance from it. Possibly, the Roshi's meaning lay in the fact that the question was also the answer. Then he would simply have to dwell upon the question.

When he reached the police station, Wainwright was waiting for him with a demand as to what in hell all this was with Beckman. "He said you assigned him to stay with the girl. Yeah, he called me. I told you we couldn't provide protection for the girl."

"It's not costing the city a cent."

"Who's paying? You? Beckman?"

"Gellman's giving us the room without charge."

"Masao, that stinks! That's taking. I run an honest force, and you're the last man in the world I'd ever accuse of taking."

"All right. If you feel that way, I'll pay for it myself."

Wainwright threw up his arms in despair. "Why? Why do you always put me on the spot?"

"I'm not trying to put you on the spot, captain. I just can't see a human being killed when I can prevent it. And as surely as the sun will come up tomorrow, I know that if he can find that girl, he'll kill her. The odds are that he will find her, but Beckman is there and I think Sy can get him first."

"Look, Masao," Wainwright said, "it's not that I don't have respect for the way you figure things. I've seen it work out too often in the past. But in this case you're guessing, and I can't go on your guesses. Morrison called me this morning. They picked up a black man who does windows down there, and they found a set of brass knucks on him and they found his fingerprints in the old lady's house. They're holding him and they're going to charge him with her murder, and that blows your theory all to hell."

"You're putting me on."

"I damn well am not! Morrison says he's going to charge him, and he feels he's got a conviction in the bag."

"I just don't believe I'm hearing this. There are possibly ten thousand sets of brass knuckles in Los Angeles, and if this black man does windows, and maybe housecleaning too, since most of them do both, his fingerprints would have to be in her house. I hate these fingerprint tricks. Has he confessed?"

"Morrison didn't mention that."

"If it were a white man, they wouldn't waste ten minutes on it. But Morrison figures he can stiff a black man and close the case and be a big hero. Well, Morrison is not only a fool, he's a malicious and meretricious fool. Any lawyer can knock that case out of court, but so help me, if it comes to a courtroom, I'll offer myself as a witness and blow Morrison's case to pieces."

"Masao, cool down! Morrison is only doing his job."

"Like hell he is! All right, I'll do something else. You gave me three days, and I'm going to hold you to your word. I'm going to hand you the killer in three days, and we'll make Los Angeles and Inglewood eat crow. Do I still have the three days? What about that?"

"You got them," Wainwright said, shaking his head hopelessly. "I said three days. You got them."

Masuto turned on his heel to leave, and Wainwright called after him, "Masao!"

"Yes?"

"Forget about paying for that room. Gellman owes us maybe a thousand parking tickets. It's time he paid off with something more than a few tickets to our annual ball."

"You're all heart," Masuto said, grinning.

"Yeah, I've been told that before."

On his way out, Masuto stopped and spoke to Polly, who ran the switchboard. She was small, very pretty, and very blond and blue-eyed, and she said plaintively, "It's nine days since you last spoke to me. What did I do wrong?"

"I've been on vacation, Polly."

"Do you know what I hate? I hate married men. I hate the institution of marriage. I hate the fact that every handsome, decent man in this town is either married or queer."

"If I believed you, I'd divorce Kati tomorrow."

"You're a liar, sergeant."

"Sometimes, yes. Look, Polly, have you ever heard of a plastic surgeon name of Leo Hartman?"

"Who hasn't?"

"Myself, for one. How old do you suppose he is?"

"Very good looking, gray hair, gray mustache. I don't know. Maybe fifty-five, maybe sixty. You can't tell with these Beverly Hills types. Maybe they do facials on each other. Professional courtesy."

"How do you know all this?"

"I read the magazines, sergeant."

"Yes, that figures. Can you get me his address?"

"Take me a moment." She riffled through the pages of a telephone book. "Here it is. Camden, between Santa Monica and Wilshire. I'll write it down for you. But don't go through with it, sergeant. You're perfect just the way you are. Don't listen to those creeps who don't like Oriental faces. I love you just the way you are."

"I'll think about it carefully," Masuto agreed.

It was only a few blocks from Rexford Drive to Camden Drive. Hartman's office was in a small, elegant medical building, and his tastefully furnished waiting room contained four ladies, none of whom, as far as Masuto could judge, was so unattractive as to require the attention of a plastic surgeon. But Masuto had discovered long ago that the only way to function as a police officer in Beverly Hills was to suspend all personal judgments and accept whatever came his way without question. He went to the little window through which Hartman's receptionist gazed out upon the waiting room, and asked to see the doctor.

"You want an appointment?"

"I want to speak to him."

"I can give you an appointment"— she consulted her day book —"oh, let us say in three weeks."

"I'm afraid I must see him immediately." Masuto

showed his badge. "I'm Detective Sergeant Masuto, Beverly Hills police. It's a matter of great urgency, and I must see him now."

"But he's with a patient."

"He's not operating, is he?"

"He does not operate here," the receptionist said scornfully. "He operates in a hospital."

"Then he can leave his patient for ten minutes. Will you please tell him that I must see him now."

She stared at Masuto, who put on his sternest look, and then she rose and disappeared. A few minutes later she opened a door at one side of the waiting room. "Follow me, please."

The doctor was waiting in his office, a large comfortable room furnished with a desk, two comfortable chairs, and several expensive potted palms. Polly's description, Masuto decided, fitted him very well, except that in Masuto's judgment, Hartman was well past sixty.

The doctor sat behind his desk, and stuffed a pipe with tobacco. "Please sit down, sergeant," he said to Masuto. "Ordinarily, nothing short of an earthquake could make me break off an examination of a patient, but Miss Weller put your case strongly. What on earth can I do for you?"

"I'll only take a few minutes of your time, and I'm very grateful that you could see me now. It is a matter of utmost urgency, and you'll forgive me if I don't explain. I have a few questions that perhaps only you can answer."

"I am puzzled, but shoot."

"We'll go back to nineteen-fifty, over thirty years ago. Could you possibly tell me who was practicing plastic surgery in that year—or would it be so large a number of physicians that you couldn't possibly name them?"

"Now hold on. It depends upon what you mean by plastic surgery. Reconstructive surgery was practiced in every hospital in southern California, but if you mean elective facial surgery, a field which to a degree centers around rhinoplasty, then that narrows the field considerably."

"Yes, that's exactly what I mean."

"Then I can help you with this area. There was Amos Cohen, over in Hollywood, Ben McKeever, here in Beverly Hills, and Fritz Lennox, who worked at the medical center in Westwood. And, of course, myself. I opened my office here in forty-six, when I came out of the army. Yes, I'm older than I look, sergeant, and as yet I've had no face-lifts. I've thought of it, but I'm too old to care, and if there's one thing a surgeon dreads, it's to have some other surgeon operate on him. Now those three men I mentioned had the field practically sewn up, if you'll forgive the pun. I know. I had the devil's own time breaking in. Of course today I could give you a list of twenty, but back then cosmetic surgery was still something of a novelty, and most of those who elected it were aging actors. Today it's different. Mothers bring me children of ten or eleven years, and there's the men, more of them every year. We live in a time when beauty skin deep has become a national obsession. By the way, it's odd that you should ask me about nineteen fifty."

"Why?"

"Because that's the year Ben McKeever died."

"How did he die?"

"Terrible tragedy, terrible. His office was in a small, frame building, over on South Spalding. Lovely place.

He had even fixed up his own operating room there, although for my part, I'll work only in a hospital. Well, it caught fire one night, and he and his nurse were burned to death. I don't suppose you'd be interested in the grisly details?"

"I would. Every detail you can remember."

"I really hate to go into it, hate to drag these things out of the past. It was pretty well hushed up at the time."

"It's of the utmost importance. Please. It will rest with me."

"Well, it would appear that he and his nurse were having an affair. Here's one reading of what happened. His nurse overdosed and died and either under the influence of some narcotic or in some insane fit of remorse, considering himself responsible for her death, he overdosed himself and set fire to the place. Now I'm not saying I believe this interpretation of the event. I knew Ben. He was a good man, and I never had any feeling that he was an addict, but who knows? Also, their bodies were badly burned, so I have doubts about the autopsy. When bodies are in a bad state, Beverly Hills autopsies could be slipshod. Then. Perhaps not now. We'll never really know what happened."

"What suggested suicide?"

"In a garbage container outside they found some hypodermic syringes which contained traces of heroin, and also a scrap of paper on which Ben had written something to the effect of, I know what I am going to do is wrong, but I am forced to do it—just about that, just a few words but enough to suggest suicide. But if he intended to write a suicide note, why was it found in the garbage? Why would he leave the syringes in the garbage? On the other hand, who is to say what a crazed man might do?"

"And I presume that all his records were burned, destroyed?"

"Yes. All of them. Why all the interest in Ben McKeever?"

"I'm sorry, I can't reveal that now. But tell me, doctor, when exactly did this happen? Even the month of the year would help."

"I can't remember the date. But I do know it was during the summer—July or August."

"Yes, that would be right. Just a few more questions and then I'll bother you no more. First of all, how completely can facial surgery change a person's appearance?"

"Well, that depends. The nose can be changed. The appearance of the eyes—to a degree. Ears can be changed. A hairlip can be corrected, but not too much can be done with a mouth. The marks of age in the neck can be removed and certain changes can be made in the cheeks. So a person's face can be changed a great deal. Of course, the art of facial cosmetic surgery is to make changes that improve without calling attention to the operation. But the shape of the head or the jaw cannot be changed."

"And if a man came to you for extensive cosmetic changes which he obviously did not need, what would you do?"

"That depends. I would try to talk him out of it if I knew something about his background. If there were any shred of reason in his request and I considered it psychologically needful, I might go along with him. If he were an actor, I might just accept his request."

"Or if he was badly scarred?"

"That would make a difference, of course."

"Or a hairlip?"

"Of course."

"And just one more thing, the other two, Cohen and Lennox—what happened to them?"

"Cohen died of a heart attack two years ago, I believe. Lennox is retired, but still alive, as far as I know."

"I've taken enough of your time," Masuto said, rising. "You've been very helpful."

"You wouldn't care to tell me what this is all about?"

"Sometime, perhaps. Not now."

8

THE MIDTOWN MANHATTAN NATIONAL BANK

Disconsolate, filled with a sense of defeat and frustration, Masuto returned to the police station on Rexford Drive, dropped into his chair, and put his arms on his desk, his chin on his hands, and brooded. Every trail came to a dead end; every gate was closed. A cold, calculating killer who destroyed without conscience or compunction. If he had murdered the doctor who changed his face and the nurse who assisted the doctor, he had planned it perfectly. Masuto could speculate that the killer had knocked them unconscious, shot heroin into them, planted the syringes, found the scrap of writing to plant in the garbage with the syringes, and then burned the house, destroying the doctor's photographs and records. From the little Masuto knew about cosmetic surgery, there was at least the knowledge that every surgeon had before and after photographs. The evidence was all gone, and with it the reputation of the two people he had killed.

Masuto prided himself on being beyond hate, yet he now felt hatred welling up within himself. He was locked in a shadowy struggle with a man who was an affront to human dignity, to conscience, to every concept of good and evil, indeed to the human race. According to Masuto's own knowledge, this man had murdered four people, four people who had done him no harm, for Masuto was certain that the skeleton under the pool had been a friend of the killer. Otherwise, how had the killer persuaded him to go there with him at night and alone?

The only thread was the girl, Rosita, and even there Masuto was beginning to have his doubts. The killer was careful. He might be quite certain that the maid had not seen him. This might very well be the end of the affair. Wednesday would come and go, and Wainwright would crack his whip.

Now it was twelve o'clock—noon, on Tuesday, and as if in answer to his thought, Wainwright entered Masuto's office, carrying two containers of coffee and two sandwiches.

"You look like hell, Masao. You look like you lost your best friend."

Masuto stared at him without answering.

"Here's coffee. I got corned beef and ham and cheese. Take your choice."

"I'm not hungry."

"That's a sorry note. I see you sitting in here like a whipped dog, and I buy you a sandwich, and you tell me you're not hungry."

"I'll have the ham and cheese."

"Good. I prefer corned beef."

"I know that."

"What in hell is it with you?" Wainwright demanded. "How do you get so damned involved in these things? You're a cop, not an avenging angel."

"I don't sleep well with a cold-blooded killer walking these streets or driving his Mercedes."

"How do you know he's walking these streets?"

"I know. Tell me, captain, if a question has no answer, the question should be enough—wouldn't you say?"

"I don't know what the hell you're talking about."

"Sit down and join me at lunch. Let's talk."

"Sure. I got nothing else to do. I just earn my pay by sitting around."

"You have to eat. I need someone to talk to."

"It takes me ten minutes to eat."

"Then let us talk for ten minutes," Masuto said, smiling.

"Okay. You got it. I'll take half your ham and cheese and give you half my corned beef. That way we can both be happy."

"No. I really prefer ham and cheese. How long have you been a cop, captain?"

"Too long. What is this?"

"Questions of crime. The question has to be the answer, I suppose, if I can find the right question."

"Twenty-two years, if you can get off that Zen kick of yours."

"Sixteen years for me. Thirty-eight years between us. A man sheds his identity. Why?"

"He killed someone. He jumped bail. He had to get out of the country."

"No, he has to stay here. That's the crux of it. He has to stay here. Or he wants to stay here."

"He's got family here."

"Come on, captain. This man doesn't give a damn about anyone."

"How do you know?"

"I know him. I know how he thinks. I know how he operates. Your ordinary criminal loses himself. This man didn't want to lose himself. He had other plans. And how did the cops know who he was? I mean, if they knew who he was, why didn't they grab him?"

"Like I said, he jumped bail."

"No, that's not his style."

"How in hell do you know what his style was?" Wainwright demanded. "Do you know how many people jump bail in any given month? Hundreds. A man knocks over a bank—"

"He's not a bank robber," Masuto interrupted. Then he leaped to his feet and grinned at Wainwright. "Of course, they were both in it. Together. God forgive my stupidity! That's why it made no sense—because I always thought of one, a loner, but to plan it and execute it right from the beginning, there had to be two of them."

"Will you calm down and tell me what the devil you are talking about?"

"No, sir. With all due respect, captain, I'm going to deliver this one to you signed, sealed, and rolled up."

"Like hell you are! I'm your boss, and I damn well want to know what's going on."

Masuto studied him, smiling slightly. "All right, we'll make a deal."

"No deals."

"Don't you want to hear what I've got to say?"

"No deals! What do you mean, you'll make me a deal?
You got one hell of a nerve, Masuto."

"Okay, you win. No deal."

"What do you mean, no deal?"

"Just that." Masuto shrugged. "The hell with it."

Now Wainwright studied Masuto shrewdly, and then
he said in a low voice, "You know what I ought to do
with you?"

"Ah, so—humbly request you fire me."

Wainwright shook his head and took the last bite of
his corned beef sandwich. "You are one painful, miserable son of a bitch, Masao. All right. What's your deal?"

"In one hour, give or take a few minutes, I will give
you the name of the killer. Not the name of the man
whose skeleton we found under the pool, but the name
of the man who killed him. I want you to know in ad-
vance that this name will do us no good—now. Maybe
later. But the killer has become someone else, the man
he killed, and that's the name we have to find."

"So you're going to give me the name of the murderer
in one hour. That's bullshit, and you know it."

"Do I make idle promises? Have you ever known me
not to deliver?"

"What's this business of two of them?"

"Do you remember what I said to you before, the
question is the answer? And then, a moment ago, you
asked me how I knew what his style is? But I know.
Why would Brody remember him? Why would Lundman remember him? Because he had a friend, a pal, a
buddy, someone close to him and with him all the time.
You don't remember one laborer; you remember two.
'I remember them,' people say, 'they were always to-

gether.' And then, once I realized that there were two of them, it made sense."

"What made sense?"

"Give me the hour, and I give you the name."

"All right, you give me the name of the killer. What do I give you?"

"Four more days. I want a week."

"You got it."

"A little more."

"I thought so. What else?"

"Travel time and expenses."

"What do you mean, travel time? Where do you have to travel?"

"I don't know yet, but I'm sure it's in the continental United States."

Wainwright stood up angrily. "You bug me, Masao. You come up with these wild guesses. You know what nobody else knows, and you're always pulling that Charlie Chan routine, grabbing things out of thin air. You promise to give me a name. How do I know it's the right name? Anyway, if I'm to believe you, the name is no damn good to us."

"Perhaps. Perhaps not."

"Great. Just great. And now you want a blank check to travel anywhere in the United States."

"Just plane fare. There and back. I promise not to stay overnight. No hotel bills. No perks."

"How come you don't know where?"

"I get that with the name of the killer."

"How can you be so damn sure?"

"Because the pieces have been floating around in my mind for three days, and finally they've come together."

Wainwright leaned back in his chair and stared at

Masuto thoughtfully. Finally, he sighed. "I don't know. I ought to be used to the way you work. All right. We got a deal. Now get me the name of the killer. In one hour. I'll be in my office."

Wainwright left the room, closing the door behind him. Masuto took a deep breath and stretched his arms. Suddenly, he felt alive, alert, filled with energy. Grudgingly—for it went against his practice of Buddhism—he admitted to himself that this was the kind of moment he embraced, the moment when ghosts ceased to be ghosts, when the quarry was almost in sight. It was embezzlement. It had to be. An ordinary thief made no sense. An ordinary thief ends up in jail or in the county graveyard. He doesn't drive a black Mercedes thirty years later. A brutal senseless murder made less sense. This man was brutal but never senseless. The only thing that fit was an embezzlement, an embezzlement large enough to justify the planning, the killing, and the apparent power of the man who drove the black Mercedes.

He picked up the telephone and buzzed Polly.

"You want a date, Masao? Any time."

"No, dear. I want the coordinating department at the F.B.I. in Washington, the place where they have all those fascinating computers."

Masuto waited, and a minute or so later, his phone rang. A voice said, "Williams, F.B.I."

"Agent Williams," he said in his most cordial tone, "this is Sergeant Masuto, Beverly Hills police. We have a problem of the most urgent nature."

"Go ahead. I'll see what we can do for you."

"I'm talking of embezzlement. In the year nineteen fifty, between the first of April and the first of May, there was a major embezzlement in a bank. No, let me put it this way, during that time the facts of a major embezzlement came to light. We would like to have as many of those facts as you can give me."

"Can you tell me anything more, sergeant? Be more definite?"

"I'm afraid not, except that we believe the sum was over a million dollars. If you have more than one in the area of that figure, I'd like to have whatever you dig up."

"All right, sergeant. I'll have to call you back to confirm, and then I'll put it through the computer. I should have something for you this afternoon."

"This afternoon?"

"You're on California time, sergeant. It's three forty-five here. I'll get you the information within the hour."

For the next half hour Masuto paced back and forth in his office. The telephone rang once, and he grabbed it eagerly. It was Sy Beckman at the hotel, to tell him that nothing had happened and he was bored to death and his Spanish was no better, and when could he go home. Masuto told him to calm down and that he would see him within an hour or so. "If I'm still a cop."

"And what does that mean?"

"I'll explain. I'll explain."

And then the telephone rang again, and it was Williams. "Masuto," he said, "I got it for you. Just one to fit your specifications in that time period, but it was a beauty. Two million eight hundred thousand dollars. How about that?"

"The only one?"

"The only one."

Masuto made notations on his pad. "What bank?"

"The Midtown Manhattan National Bank, upper Madison Avenue in New York. The culprit was the chief teller, name of Stanley Cutler." He spelled it out. "Twenty-five years old, Caucasian, American born, veteran with two decorations. Orphan, raised in a Buffalo orphanage, IQ of a hundred and thirty-seven, no priors. Honorable discharge, November nineteen forty-five, went to work at the Midtown Manhattan in January of forty-six, trained as a teller and rose rapidly. The embezzlement began during April, nineteen forty-nine, but wasn't discovered until an audit a year later. Classified as a brilliant piece of work, an innovation in bank embezzlement. By the way, what's your interest in this out there?"

"You'll receive a full report within the week."

"Well, the file is open, even after thirty years. No trace ever of Cutler or a nickel of the two million eight. If you've got anything, let us know."

"I certainly will. Do you have pictures and prints?"

"Both. I can wire you both and then send you a glossy through the mail."

"By the way, Williams, how tall was Cutler?"

"Five eight and a half."

"Can you send me a full description, eye color, hair, everything you have? Care of Sergeant Masao Masuto, Rexford Drive, Beverly Hills, 90210."

"Right. What are you, Masuto, Japanese?"

"That's right."

"Poetic justice if you catch up with Cutler. He fought in the Pacific."

"So it goes."

"Good luck."

Masuto put down the telephone, took a sheet from his pad, and printed in block letters STANLEY CUTLER. He then went into Wainwright's office.

"The hour's almost up," Wainwright told him.

"Not quite." He put the sheet of paper on the desk in front of Wainwright.

"What's this?"

"The name of our killer."

"Who the devil is Stanley Cutler?"

"I haven't the vaguest idea. I only know that he murdered six people."

"Six? Where do you get six?"

"The man under the pool. A doctor named Ben Mc-Keever, his nurse, the two Lundmans and Mrs. Brody. The doctor and his nurse are pure guesswork, so we may have to scrap those two."

"Who the hell is Ben McKeever?"

"I'll tell you about it, captain. By the way, I'm flying to New York tonight on the red eye. It's the cheapest flight."

"It would be New York," Wainwright said sourly.

9

BLIND
ALLEYS

Masuto called Beckman at the Beverly Glen Hotel, and after listening to Beckman's woeful description of the state of his marriage, informed him that some respite was imminent. "You can leave her for a few hours. Have you had lunch?"

"Just finished."

"Then tell her to lock and bolt the door, and not to open it for anyone except you. Not for anyone. Make a simple code word between you, just in case she's too frightened to recognize your voice. Then get over here to the station."

"Will you talk to my wife?"

"I'll talk to her."

But talking to Sophie Beckman was not easy, and Masuto waited patiently to get a word in. "What do you mean, secrets?" she demanded. "What am I, the town crier? He can't tell me where he is or what he's doing? You're supposed to be cops, but you're beginning to sound like those creeps at the C.I.A. who won't tell Congress what they're doing, even if what they're doing is planning to blow up the world, which would be all right, but you're dealing with my husband who can't keep his eyes off any woman under ninety who comes by, and about his hands, I won't even mention—"

She paused for a breath, and Masuto said quickly, "I give you my word, Sophie, this is his assignment, and it's legitimate."

"For how long? When do I see him again?"

"Another day or two."

"Not that I'm breaking my heart to see him, Masao, but it's the way I'm treated."

"He's more miserable than you are."

"I hope so."

"Just another day or two, Sophie."

"Is he with a woman?"

"Absolutely not."

"You're lying, Masao. I could draw you a picture of the woman he's with—an oversized blonde with big boobs—"

"What did you say, Sophie?" Masuto asked with sudden excitement.

"I said I could draw you a picture—"

"Yes, of course. No, no, you're misjudging Sy. He's doing a hard and arduous job, believe me."

Finally, he managed to calm her, fortunately, since while he was talking to her, an officer entered and put a telephoto on his desk.

"For you, sergeant, with the compliments of the F.B.I."

Masuto stared at the picture, recalling with some

guilt the times in the past when he had been less than generous in his opinion of the Federal Bureau of Investigation. He had to admit now that if less than long on simple intelligence, when it came to the keeping of files and the use of computers, they were without peer. Wire photos are not of the best, nevertheless it was with great excitement that he stared at the photo of the man ‑he hunted. Thirty years had passed since this picture was taken. He saw the face of a young man, most likely blond or with light brown hair, with pale eyes, a long, thin nose, a mole prominent on one cheek, a wide jaw, fleshy cheeks, heavy brows that almost met over the nose, and thin lips. There was a scar along the left side of the jawbone.

For at least five minutes he sat immobile, staring at the photo. Then he picked it up and went into Wainwright's office, where he laid the picture on the desk in front of the captain.

"What's this?" Wainwright asked.

"Our murderer, thirty years ago. Mr. Stanley Cutler, in the flesh."

"Where did you get this?"

"Courtesy of the F.B.I."

"Masao, if this is another one of your ploys—"

"That's our man. Thirty years ago, he embezzled two million eight hundred thousand dollars from the Midtown Manhattan National Bank. That's how the F.B.I. came into it. They never found him or the money."

"Where does it connect? You're guessing again."

"Am I? Perhaps. But every instinct in my body tells me I'm right. This is the way I spell it out. The embezzlement took place over twelve months. He had a partner, whom he set up from the very beginning for the kill. That's the way his mind works."

"How the hell do you know how his mind works?"

"I told you before that I know him. Just ride with it. He needs the partner to open bank accounts, to spread the money around, maybe to buy various bearer bonds, governments, municipals. Conceivably, the partner comes to California, stashes the loot here. They take a whole year. I was going to New York to see the people at the bank and find out exactly how he did it, but that's not important now."

"You mean you're not going to New York?"

"No, something came up."

"What?"

"This picture. Anyway, it's thirty years. Who knows if there's anyone alive who can give me the information?"

"If this is our man, let's spread the picture around."

"No good, captain. It was thirty years ago. I told you he had his face done."

"What about his prints? Get them from the feds. They don't change. He worked in a bank. They got to have his prints."

"Maybe. They didn't come through." Masuto smiled. "If they do, it won't matter. He took care of things like that."

"How do you take care of prints?"

"There are ways, believe me. If a man is tough enough, he can burn them off."

"So what it amounts to is that you have nothing. You have his picture and his name, and you got nothing. Not one shred of evidence. Masao, I ought to have my head examined. I've put two men on the payroll of the City of Beverly Hills to work chasing ghosts, and I've damn near talked you into making me believe in your ghosts."

"I've called off the New York trip. That's a boost to your budget."

"All right. What do you get in exchange?"

"I want you to call Kennedy and make peace with him and borrow his police artist for tomorrow."

"Why?"

"Because we can't afford a police artist of our own," Masuto said gently.

"That's very funny. You know, Masao, there are people who tell me the Japanese don't have a sense of humor. They're wrong. You let me talk the city manager into sending a man to New York, and now you don't have to go to New York. That's funny too. You just about tell Captain Kennedy that he's a horse's ass, and now you want me to talk him out of his police artist. That's even funnier."

"Give him a deal. Quid pro quo. He lends us the artist, we give him the murderer of the Lundmans."

"Masao," Wainwright said seriously, "I have more respect for you than you might imagine. We've worked together a good many years now, and I've seen you pull more rabbits out of the hat than you can shake a stick at. I'm even ready to believe that this is a photograph of the killer. But you still got nothing, not a shred of evidence, not one bit of anything I can bring to the D.A. That is, considering that you could find Stanley Cutler. I know you don't have a high opinion of the feds, but they got maybe the biggest facility in the world, and they've been looking for Cutler these thirty years, and they have come up with zilch. Maybe Cutler's dead, maybe in Brazil, and it's still not beyond the realm of possibility that some lunatic killed the Lundmans. God knows, there are plenty of them."

"The Lundmans and Mrs. Brody in one day—that would be stretching coincidence too far."

"It happens."

"No, I can't accept that."

"What then, Masao? You want me to promise Kennedy that we'll wrap this up and deliver him his culprit. Then we wash out. Where does that leave me?"

"You're right," Masao said after a moment. "You can't promise that. But I need that artist."

"Okay, I'll try."

He went back to his office. Beckman was waiting for him, and the telephone was ringing as Masuto entered. It was Williams, calling from Washington. "I'm sorry, Masuto," he said, "but we don't have prints."

"You'd better explain that."

"During the war Cutler pulled a man out of a burning tank. Seared his fingers. Got a citation for it."

"What about prints when he went into the army?"

"He joined up in Europe. There are no prints, Masuto, there just aren't any. Now look, if you people have a lead on Cutler, we want him."

"What about the statute of limitations?"

"There's none on retrieving the money, and we'll let the lawyers worry about the rest."

"Hold on a moment," Masuto said. "Do you have anything on that soldier he pulled out of the tank? Did he recover? His name? Anything?"

"We thought of that. No way we could trace him."

"Wouldn't his name be on the citation?"

"Not necessarily. There were witnesses to the incident. That's all you need for the citation."

Masuto put down the telephone and turned to Beckman. "We have a beauty, Sy. We have a brilliant psychopath who goes in for perfect crimes. Your average criminal has an IQ of ninety or ninety-five. Cutler's IQ is one hundred and thirty-seven. He climbed into a burning tank to save a G.I. and seared his ten fingers. At this point, I'm ready to believe he did it consciously and purposefully."

"That's crazy, Masao. No one burns himself on purpose."

"No? Perhaps not. Will the girl keep the door locked?"

"Right. She's scared enough. Did you square me with Sophie?"

"I think so. Now here's where we are, Sy. I'm going to lay out everything we have."

When Masuto had finished spelling out what he had from Williams and whatever other pieces he had put together, Beckman stared at the picture and shook his head. "What does it add up to, Masao? A picture thirty years old of a man who had facial surgery, a name that doesn't belong to him anymore, and no fingerprints. That's a stacked deck. Suppose you find him? How do you prove his identity? With Lundman dead, how do you tie him into a crime that happened thirty years ago? As far as the Lundmans are concerned, there's a perfect murder. No weapon, no witnesses."

"Except Rosita."

"Come on, Masao. She wasn't a witness. You know that. The D.A. would laugh at it."

"You're sure she's all right until five o'clock?"

"Unless he can walk through a steel door."

"That wouldn't surprise me either. Now I'll tell you what we're going to do. We're going to visit banks, not the branches, but the main offices. Here's the way I worked this out. I believe that Cutler planned this for years. He got out of the army and got himself a job in a bank. Meanwhile, he had worked out a pattern of embezzlement. That wouldn't be too hard for a man of his caliber. There are plenty of books on the great embezzlements, and in those days they were going out of their way to give jobs to vets—especially vets who had won decorations. Cutler had a partner. For some reason, I believe, Cutler selected Los Angeles for his ultimate goal, perhaps because it was the other side of the continent, more likely because most of the money in L.A. is new money. Now Cutler had a problem. Money is a problem. Two or three million dollars is a huge problem."

"I should have that kind of a problem."

"Still a problem. What do you do with it? You can't keep it under a mattress. So the way I see it, Cutler had a partner, a loyal, devoted partner who obeyed orders and who trusted Cutler with his life."

"And who ended up under the swimming pool."

"Exactly. How he got this partner we may never know. Possibly the man whose life he saved. In any case, Cutler would have chosen someone his size with the same eye and hair color, so that the driver's license and everything else would fit. Cutler funneled the money through him; it would have been too risky to try to do it himself. I imagine that for the most part they bought bonds, government bonds, company bonds, municipal bonds, all as good as cash. His partner could open accounts in half a dozen brokerage houses, and they spread their winnings over a year. But at the same time, a man like Cutler would see to it that they had some cash resources at their destination—namely L.A. At least that's my guess. I'm trying to think the way he thinks, and by now I have a pretty good notion of how he thinks. Perhaps his partner made two or three trips to Los Angeles, and each time he'd open a few bank accounts—nothing spectacular, perhaps ten thousand here, five thousand there. His partner must have been overwhelmed at the way Cutler trusted him to open the accounts in his own name, but at the same time he was signing his death warrant. Again, we'll never know how Cutler persuaded John Doe to sign on that job as a day laborer. Maybe it was simply a way to drop out of sight. You don't look for a high-class embezzler on a construction job. But persuade him he did, and there he saw the opportunity to get rid of John Doe forever, and he took it."

"And you figure we might get lucky and find two or three bank accounts for the same name?"

"It's a long shot."

"Too long, Masao. Thirty years too long."

Masuto stared at him for a moment, then he picked up the telephone and asked Polly to get him the manager at the central office of the Los Angeles branch of the Crocker Bank. The phone rang, and Masuto picked it up, introduced himself, and stated his case. The man at the Crocker Bank, whose name was Johnson, sighed deeply and said, "I'm afraid not, sergeant."

"Why not?"

"Because thirty years is just too long. We do have a central storage depot and we do have a great deal of material on microfilm, but to be able to find and compare the names of small depositors in nineteen fifty or in nineteen forty-nine—well, I'm just afraid it's impossible."

"How impossible?"

"Impossible, sir. Well, let me be honest. I'm not absolutely sure that those records don't exist. I would have to go to our central office in San Francisco for full information. Then someone would have to spend days going through the microfilm—providing the records have been kept. We do keep records of our own accounting over that period, but names of depositors? Most unlikely. But let me say this. Give me the name of the depositor, and I'll try to track it down."

"I don't have the name of the depositor."

"What? Are you trying to make a fool of me, sir? Is this really the Beverly Hills police?"

"You can call back if you wish. This is the Beverly Hills police. We are trying to find out whether the same name appears in several banks."

"Without knowing the name?"

"The fact of the duplication would establish the name."

"Sergeant, you're wasting my time. It's impossible."

Masuto looked at Beckman and nodded.

"What did he say?"

"He says it's impossible."

"I thought so. The L.A.P.D. might cover something like that, if they could put twenty men on it and take a month. We're too small, and who knows if the records exist? You want me to try another bank?"

"No, it wouldn't be any different."

"So what's left?"

"Rosita, the police artist, and, I think, my kinsman, Ishido."

"Who is Ishido?"

"He is Kati's father's cousin. He was an officer in the Japanese Imperial Army, and he has lived in Los Angeles these past thirty-three years. He has enormous interests in Mitsubishi and Sony, and before he retired he represented Mitsubishi on the West Coast. He is also Samurai, which may not mean much here, but still counts among the folk from the old country. Now he collects Japanese stamps and Chinese jade. He has more millions than we have fingers between us, and since he is what he is, and I am a policeman, you can imagine that he does not look too kindly upon me. I sometimes think that he has never forgiven Kati for marrying me. On the few occasions when I have seen him, he has been very courteous, but that's his manner."

"And you figure him as a connection?"

"I hope so."

"So we washed out with the banks. What do I do now?"

"Go back to the lovely Rosita."

"You know," Beckman said, "you are putting a large temptation in the face of an ordinary cop. I am human, Masao, and that kid is just too damn pretty."

"Exercise restraint."

"If Sophie ever found out, she'd cut my throat."

"We'll try to keep it a secret." And then, as Beckman was about to leave, Masuto said, "Sy, if Cutler should get on to us and somehow get into that room with you, use your gun. Don't try to take him and put cuffs on him. Use your gun, even if he's unarmed. Shoot out a kneecap or something."

"What? Are you crazy?"

"At this point, I don't know."

"He's five eight. I'm twice his size. I've never met the man I couldn't take, and I don't go for that karate crap."

"This might be the first time."

"I'll think about it."

When Beckman had left, Masuto went into Wainwright's office and stood waiting.

"Yeah," Wainwright said. "I did it."

"We get the police artist?"

"He'll be over here at ten o'clock tomorrow."

"Captain, you're wonderful."

"Yeah. Well, it's your turn to be Mr. Wonderful. Pick up a box of one dollar Flaminco cigars. Make sure they're genuine Flamincos and that they come from the Canary Islands, wherever they are. There are twenty in a box, so it will cost you twenty bucks."

"What for?"

"For Kennedy. It's part of the deal."

Masuto went back to his office and called Dr. Leo Hartman. "I would like to see you tomorrow," he said, "at about noon."

"That's impossible, sergeant."

"Yes, I've spent the day hearing that things were impossible. Let me put it this way, Dr. Hartman. You indicated that Ben McKeever was a man you admired. Perhaps I can tell you that he was murdered and his nurse was murdered. If you will give me an hour of your time tomorrow, it's possible I can bring in his killer."

"My God, sergeant, that was thirty years ago."

"His killer is still alive, free, and prosperous. Is it worth an hour of your time?"

"Are you being serious?"

"Very serious."

"All right. Come in at twelve fifteen. I can give you forty-five minutes. Will that be enough?"

"I think so."

"I'll have some sandwiches sent in. Have you any preference?"

"Whatever you choose will be fine. I'll be bringing another man with me."

"I hope you're right, sergeant. It was an ignominious way to die."

Masuto met Wainwright on his way out, and the captain asked him where he was off to.

"Home," Masuto said.

"It's only half past four. You're making an early day of it."

"I got home at nine yesterday."

"You're a cop."

"Sy's wife is talking about divorcing him. Do you want Kati to divorce me?"

"I hear your people don't go in for divorce."

"So you hear."

"I got three burglaries and a mugging. Right here in Beverly Hills. A car pulls up next to this lady's car. Two guys jump out, open the doors, grab her purse, and drive off."

"She should lock her doors."

"All right. I gave you the week. I regret it, but I gave it to you."

10
THE POLICE
ARTIST

A few minutes before the police artist arrived the following morning, the postman brought in a glossy photo of Stanley Cutler, which Williams had dispatched by express mail. The police artist arrived a few minutes before ten, a young man of about thirty, tall, redheaded, and with a Texas accent. "Well now," he said in a soft drawl, "I am mighty pleased to meet you. I'm Kenny Dawson, and you are Sergeant Masuto. I did suspect from your name that you would be some kind of Oriental. Japanese? Am I right?"

"You're right, Mr. Dawson."

"Now don't call be Mr. Dawson, sergeant. Kenny will do. I hear you got a problem that wants an artist? Of course, I would think that in a place like Beverly Hills, which I hear has more millionaires per square mile than any other spot in the U.S. of A., they would have a police artist of their own."

"We don't have call for one very often. Are you good, Kenny?"

"Good enough. Gotta admit that I put aside my dreams of being another Frederic Remington for a steady job, but that don't mean I have sold out. Now what have you got for me?"

Masuto handed him the glossy print of Stanley Cutler. "This picture was taken about thirty years ago. As you can see, it's probably an identity photo for a job record."

"Sure enough. Same technique as passport photos."

"I want you to draw it, but to change it to conform to thirty years of aging. I can tell you that the man has not gained much weight. He stays in good physical condition. Do you think you can do that?"

"I'll give it a try. You don't have a profile, do you?"

"Just this. And we have an hour and a half. Is that enough time?"

"Plenty."

"And one thing more," Masuto added. "Can you use a medium where you can erase and make changes?"

"Sure. I'll use charcoal without fixing it, and then we can pick it up with a kneaded eraser." He looked at Masuto curiously. "By the way, you wouldn't like to explain what I'm doing?"

"Well, you're doing what few men get to do, compressing thirty years in an hour, and then we're going to consult a plastic surgeon."

"Yes, that answers my question."

The telephone rang. It was Williams, calling from Washington, and he asked about the glossy print.

"We got it. Thanks for the cooperation."

"By the way, sergeant," Williams said, "there's a ten

percent finder's fee on the two million eight hundred thousand. Of course, the bank was paid off by the insurance company. That's Transwest National Insurance. They put the finder's fee on it back in nineteen fifty. I spoke to them this morning, and they say the fee is still in force, a very neat two hundred and eighty thousand dollars. Inflation puts a bite into it, but it's still a nice piece of change."

Wainwright was scowling at some papers on his desk when Masuto came into his office and sat down facing him.

"You got nothing to do," Wainwright said. "You and Beckman, you really stiffed me. He's shacked up with some cute Mexican babe, and you got nothing to do but sit here in my office with that Charlie Chan look on your face."

"So sorry, but the artist is at work, and meanwhile Agent Williams called from the Federal Bureau of Investigation, and he tells me the Transwest National Insurance Company put a ten percent finder's fee on that two million eight embezzlement, and while thirty years has passed, the finder's fee is still in force."

"You got to be kidding."

"Oh, no. No, indeed."

"Masao, bums who pull off these jobs spend it quicker than you could walk to the bank."

"Two million eight hundred thousand dollars?"

"It's thirty years."

"Let's just suppose, captain, that this particular bum has other plans. He wants to be rich and powerful. The embezzlement money is his stake. He nurtures it, invests it. Possibly he goes into some business. These last thirty years have been very rewarding here in southern California. Today he has millions."

"Still at it, Masao?"

"Suppose I'm right? All we have to do is to identify him."

"If we can't convict him for murder—and I don't see a chance of a snowball in hell that we can—then the statute of limitations has run out in the embezzlement, and he can walk around and thumb his nose at us, that is considering that you ever find him."

"Oh, I'll find him," Masuto said. "As far as criminal action is concerned, you may be right that we can't touch him. But suppose the money can be reclaimed in a civil suit? After all, there's no statute of limitations on stolen property. I read where they're still litigating World War Two disputes, and that's forty years ago."

"You may have a point there. But don't get any notions about becoming a rich cop. If it ever came to that, the money would go to the City of Beverly Hills."

"It might get us that ten percent raise we've been asking for."

"I doubt it."

"Well, one step at a time, captain. By tonight I expect to know who Stanley Cutler is."

"It's Wednesday," Wainwright said. "I expected as much."

"I'm sure," Masuto said dryly.

When Masuto returned to his office, Dawson was completing the charcoal portrait. Very skillfully, he had aged the portrait, pushing back the hairline, allowing the cheeks to expand and sag a bit, putting wrinkles around the eyes, lines on the brow and around the mouth, and loose flesh and folds of skin on the neck.

"That's very good," Masuto said.

"No, it isn't. Any art student could do as well."

"I doubt it."

"You should see my paintings. All this crap about naturalism and photorealism that's coming up now. I was doing it ten years ago, when I was just a kid. But you want to know about the art scene in Los Angeles? It stinks. A few lousy galleries on La Cienega, a couple in Beverly Hills that are even lousier. New York's the place, but they tell me you got to pay six, seven hundred a month for some small, rundown loft in Soho. I need a stake. You don't know any of the local art collectors, do you, sergeant?"

"I'm afraid not."

"Well, who does? Anyway, here it is. What do we do now?"

"We go to see Dr. Leo Hartman."

"You want me to drag all my stuff with me?"

"You might as well. You have fixative?"

"What am I—an amateur?"

"Good. I'll want to fix the drawing when we finish there."

In Masuto's car Dawson said, "The way I got it figured is this. This character ripped off something important thirty years ago and you're after him now. It had to be a homicide, otherwise the statute of limitations would have wiped it out. I would be mighty pleased to be let in on your secret, Sergeant Masuto."

"Sorry. You'll just have to be patient and read about it in the papers."

"I don't read the papers, sergeant. It's too depressing. I watch the news on TV with a pad, and I draw everything I see. That's what's responsible for the whole decay of the art scene. Nobody knows how to draw anymore. No standards. To me drawing is like playing the piano. You just have to stick with it every day of your life or you lose it."

Hartman kept them waiting for half an hour before he was ready to see them, during which time Dawson attempted to sketch one of the women sitting in the waiting room and was told in no uncertain terms that she had not come there to be an artist's model. He contented himself with sketching Masuto, and had achieved a fair likeness when the receptionist told them that the doctor could see them now.

In Hartman's office Masuto introduced Dawson while the doctor unwrapped sandwiches.

"Mighty kind of you," Dawson said. "I didn't expect lunch to come with it."

"My contribution to the good cause," Hartman said.

Masuto placed the glossy photograph of Cutler on Hartman's desk. "This is the man who may have murdered Ben McKeever. This picture of him was taken perhaps thirty-three years ago, when he went to work at the Midtown Manhattan National Bank. It's not the best picture in the world, but it's all we have. That appears to have been a rather bad scar on his jaw, possibly a war wound. Now Dawson, here, has drawn his likeness as he might appear today. Of course there's guesswork on Dawson's part, but it's a beginning. Here is what I would like you to do, doctor, if you will be so kind. The man in the photo comes into your office, as he came into McKeever's office. I don't know what went on there, and probably we never will know. But the fact is that he persuaded McKeever to change his face. Now just for the sake of our experiment, let us imagine that you are in McKeever's place. This man comes into your office and he persuades you to change his face. Now I know nothing about your practice, but I suspect that both you and McKeever would follow somewhat the same procedure. Or are there many alternatives?"

Hartman was studying the photograph. "No, not too many alternatives. Perhaps none. Is this the only picture?"

"As I said, the only one."

"If we only had a profile. But we haven't, have we."

"Here is Dawson's drawing."

Hartman put down the glossy and stared at the drawing. "It's damn good."

"Is it a reasonable reconstruction of the aging process?"

"Fairly so. I think you've made the neck too scrawny. The photo shows a very muscular neck. I would guess that he would wear a sixteen and a half or a seventeen shirt. Age would add flesh to it, and there would be some horizontal lines under the chin."

"He is a man who stays in excellent physical condition," Masuto said.

"Oh?" Hartman looked at him thoughtfully. "May I ask how you know that if you don't know who he is?"

"In time. Could we get back to the photo? He comes into your office. You agree to change his face. What would you do?"

Hartman turned to Dawson. "How long would it take you to make a tracing of this photo—a line drawing but with all the features and marks?"

"About five minutes."

"Do it. Meanwhile we'll eat. You see," he said to Masuto, taking a bite out of his sandwich, "there is not too much you can do with the human face. We're not molding in clay. We work with flesh and bone. It's very popular in novels and movies for the criminal to go to a plastic surgeon and order a new face. It really can't be done. Now during the war I was a young surgeon in the Pacific, and since then I've done a great deal of work with people who are badly burned or injured in car crashes. In such cases, you very often do build a completely new face, but only because the old face has been destroyed, and in such cases the countenance is never quite normal."

"Why couldn't McKeever have done this with him?"

"Smash his face? Burn it? No, sergeant, we don't do such things. Cosmetic surgery is limited, thank God."

Dawson finished the tracing and handed it to the doctor. He laid it on his desk with the photograph beside it. "Suppose you change the neck on your drawing, and let me study these for a few minutes."

For the next few minutes Hartman munched his sandwich and studied the tracing and the photo. Then he said to Dawson, "Move around so you can see what I'm doing. Then you make the changes in your drawing."

"Okay, Doc. Got you."

"First thing, we get rid of the scar." He made marks on the tracing.

"Can you do that and show no new scars?" Masuto asked.

"If you're good, and Ben McKeever was good."

"Heavier neck and no scar," Dawson said.

"Get rid of the mole."

"Done."

"Now, in getting rid of the scar, we make this incision on the other side of the jaw, cut here and here, and lo and behold we've changed the shape of his mouth."

"How much?" Dawson asked.

"Just a trifle." He made the change on his tracing. "But see how it changes his appearance. A rather petulant look, but his face would light up more when he smiles. It might give him a charming smile, and I suppose that with his nature, that would be an asset. Now the nose, and there's the problem. The most prominent feature on man's face, the nose. If we only had a profile. Do you know his name?" he asked Masuto.

"Is that important?"

"It might be."

"Cutler. Stanley Cutler."

"Anglo-Saxon. Or Irish, conceivably. Irish would account for that long, pointed nose—straight, long, and pointed. We'll bob it, very simple, done it a hundred times. Here, young fellow." He made the change on his tracing, and carefully using his kneaded eraser, Dawson changed the drawing to conform.

"Ah, now we're beginning to see what the devil looks like. Now, one more simple detail, and we'll have Mr. Cutler with a face that even his own mother wouldn't recognize. Of course, that's just an expression," he explained to Masuto. "His mother might recognize him, but she'd want to know what he had done to himself. Then again, maybe she wouldn't. I think if I were doing the job, she wouldn't."

"That one more simple detail?" Dawson suggested.

"Oh, yes. Yes, indeed. You see the way his brows come together? That's perhaps the most noticeable feature on his face, that heavy line right across his brow. Well, we separate the brows. Remove a piece here, remove a piece here, and then, if we're doing a really artistic job, we lessen the thickness of what remains by about a quarter of an inch. Like this." He made the change on the tracing and pushed it over to Dawson. "See what he's become? He's no longer a sullen, miserable creature. He's quite sensitive, isn't he? The inquiring mind. Isn't it marvelous what a raised brow will do? A trick actors learned long ago. There you are. Mc-Keever has given him a new face, a new look, a new character, and he could walk through the corridors of any police department in perfect security."

"And you could do all this?" Masuto asked. "The man's face would reveal no sign of it, no scars at all?"

"For the first few months the scars would show. After all, the trauma to the skin and flesh has been very severe."

"How long?"

"Five, six, seven months. But they are fading. By now, all trace should be gone, even to close examination."

"Is it possible for fingerprints to disappear with burns on the fingertips?"

"Yes, indeed. And even without severe burns, if one does work of a certain kind. Great mythology about fingerprints. But you have aroused my curiosity enormously. When do you expect to arrest this man?"

"As soon as I find him," Masuto replied, knowing it was hardly that simple. "You've helped us enormously."

"It's been fascinating. Both of you very interesting."

He handed a card to Dawson. "Keep in touch. I use an artist quite often, and the work pays. Give me a call next week." And to Masuto he said, "I have stifled my curiosity, but a Nisei detective on our little police force, I must say I like the notion."

"It's interesting work," Masuto said for want of anything else to say.

Outside, Dawson said, "So it goes. Art for art's sake. From police artist to the reconstruction of the faces of rich dames. I wonder what he pays?"

"Ask him."

"Right. What do you think, sergeant, am I worth twenty dollars an hour?"

"Every bit of it."

"It's not what they pay me at the L.A.P.D., but this is Beverly Hills, isn't it?"

"It certainly is."

"You got kids, sergeant?"

"Two of them."

"Well, if they want to be artists, discourage them. My uncle's a rancher, but I saw cows branded once, and that was the end of it for me. I'll ride back to your office with you and fix the drawing, and then if you're finished with me, I'll take in some of those lousy galleries on La Cienega. Might as well see what the competition is doing."

After Dawson had left, Masuto took the charcoal drawing into Wainwright and spread it out on his desk.

"What's this?"

"Stanley Cutler."

"Is this what you needed the police artist for? It doesn't even resemble the photo you showed me."

"No? Well, it's thirty years later and he's had a lot of cosmetic surgery."

Wainwright grinned and shook his head. "You are wonderful, Masao. I don't know what the hell to make of you, but you are something." He stared at the drawing again. "On the other hand, I could swear that I've seen this man somewhere."

"It's rather unique, isn't it?" Masuto said. "We discover the skeleton of a man murdered thirty years ago. The murderer has killed five other people. We know his name, and I think we know what he looks like and tonight I suspect I will know who he is, and we can't touch him."

"So you've come to that conclusion too?"

"I'm afraid so."

"Well, there it is," Wainwright said. "It happens. I think it happens a lot more than the public suspects. There's a lot of killers, a lot of criminals walking around on the streets, and the cops know it, and the cops can't touch them."

"I still have to know who he is."

"Why? What good will it do? You can't tie him into any of the murders. You can't even tie him into the embezzlement, because if he has no prints and his face is changed, there's no way ever to prove that he's Stanley Cutler."

"Don't forget," Masuto said, "that he has taken the name of the man he put under the swimming pool."

"So you say. Guesses. He could take any name. In the right places here in L.A. you can buy a social security card and a birth certificate, not to mention honorable

discharge papers. So why stay with the name of the man
he killed?"

"Because it gives him roots, a place of origin, a home-
town. This man didn't want to lose himself. He wanted
to be a man of position and power. Those are his gods,
wealth and power, and to have those things, he has killed
without mercy."

Wainwright looked at him long and thoughtfully.
"You know, Masao," he finally said, "we've been together a lot of years. If you weren't Nisei, you'd be
running this police force, although with your mind, I
never understood why you wanted to be a cop. I know,"
he continued, waving a hand, "it's your karma. Only I
don't buy that. I don't buy one little bit of it. It's something else. I've watched you through a lot of cases, and
particularly through this. And most of the time, I keep
my mouth shut and give you a free hand. So this time
I kept my mouth shut, which maybe I shouldn't have
done." He tapped the drawing on his desk. "You've
gone to a lot of effort. You figured out what kind of a
crime led to that murder up on Laurel Way. You tracked
it down. You got yourself a suspect. You got his name
and background and you got a picture of what he might
look like if he were alive today—and to get this picture
you had to tie in a plastic surgeon and his nurse. But I've
been asking around about Dr. Ben McKeever. Masao, he
was an addict, and his nurse was an addict, and he had
fouled up his life from A to Z. You took what Leo
Hartman told you for gospel. Well, I don't know what
the relationship between Hartman and McKeever was,
but either Hartman was taken in by McKeever, or he

was covering. Well, that's all right. McKeever was a middle-aged man and Hartman was just starting out, so maybe McKeever threw him some bones, so to speak."

"Where did you get all this?" Masuto asked him.

"Where do you think? I called Chief Maddox, who ran the police force thirty years ago. He's almost eighty, but he has all his buttons, and he told me the circumstances. They were having an affair. The nurse's name was Mary Clancy. One of her kids smashed up a car and was killed. Mary overdosed and died. McKeever called the cops. When they got there, the house was in flames. The dirty stuff was hushed up. So this picture doesn't mean one damn thing."

"I think it does," Masuto said slowly. "It's been in back of my mind since I called the F.B.I. It's been there, and I kept chasing it away."

"What's been there?"

"Just a notion. I chase it away, and it comes back and reverses everything. Let's suppose that John Doe is Stanley Cutler, that it's Stanley Cutler's skeleton that we found under the pool, that his partner planned and executed the whole thing. Then there would be no need for concealment on the killer's part, and no way to connect him with the embezzlement. He put Cutler into the bank, showed him how to operate, and then, when the proper moment arrived, killed him."

"Then if you thought of this, why this whole business of the police artist?"

"Because I don't know. You're telling me that McKeever was in neck deep. All the more reason why he should do business with a man like Cutler. If he called the police, he could have done so at the point of a gun. But maybe that's all a surmise with no foundation. Do

124

you want me to drop it at this point? You're the boss. You've been needling me about dropping it. Do you really want me to?"

Wainwright stared at Masuto for a long moment, and then he said, "Goddamnit, no! That murder thirty years ago was on our turf. I want you to find the bastard and bring him in."

11

ISHIDO

Even Masuto, who could look at the enormous wealth and very conspicuous consumption of Beverly Hills with objectivity and without envy, related to his wife's kinsman, Ishido, with awe. It was not simply that Ishido's wealth was larger than most Beverly Hills wealth; it was the way Ishido was. Whereas visitors to Beverly Hills have often noted that it specializes in vulgarity, Ishido epitomized taste. Actually, Ishido did not live in Beverly Hills, but a few miles to the west in Bel-Air, a neighborhood with a little more posh and perhaps a good deal more money than Beverly Hills. There Ishido lived alone —his wife having died seven years before—in a large, single-story Japanese-style house, surrounded by green hedges, a brick wall, and patrolled by two armed guards and two Doberman pinschers. Ishido himself was a small, deceptively gentle and pleasant man of some sixty-five years. At the age of twenty-five he had been a colonel in the Imperial Japanese Army. When the war ended, he was the youngest general in the army. He had come to California in 1947 to represent one of the new Japanese companies that were rising out of the ruins left by the war, and now, thirty-three years later, he was retired, a multi-millionaire, and a quiet power in the Los Angeles area.

Ishido had come from a moderately important Samurai family; but moderately important or not, his was still Samurai. Masuto's father had been a gardener; and Kati remembered this as Masuto finished his dinner and headed for the door.

"Masao," she called softly.

He paused and turned to her.

"You are going to see Ishido?"

"Yes, I told you so. It's no great joy, but I have to see him. I don't know who else can help me now."

"Like that? The way you are dressed?"

He was wearing his brown tweed jacket and gray flannel trousers. The jacket was two years old and the trousers were wrinkled. He wore a white shirt without a tie and open at the neck. His brown shoes were scuffed and needed shining.

"This is the way I dress," Masuto said with annoyance. "I am a policeman, a cop. Ishido knows that. He has been kind enough to see me on very short notice—insufferably kind—and I have no intention of deluding him with the notion that a Beverly Hills cop can afford to buy his clothes at Carroll's," he said, referring to the fine men's shop at the corner of Rodeo and Santa Monica.

"But you might well convince him," Kati said, smiling, "that a Beverly Hills cop has a wife who can press trousers most excellently."

"Would it make you happy?"

"Please."

Masuto took off his trousers, and sat glumly and un-happily in his underwear in the kitchen. When his son and daughter glanced in and began to titter, he snapped at them angrily.

"What has come over you?" Kati asked.

"I have reached a point where I can conceal my igno-rance from everyone but myself."

"Oh, Masao, the things you say!"

"Why didn't I trust myself? I sensed it from the be-ginning. There were two men. One was strong, demonic, aggressive, pathological. The other was weak and malle-able. Kati, if Cutler were the strong man, there would have been no need for him to kill Lundman. Because if he were Cutler, his face would have been changed, his fingerprints absent—then how could anyone identify him or accuse him? But the other man, John Doe, he was not wanted by the F.B.I. No one was looking for him—unless Lundman or Mrs. Brody remembered. And do you know why they would remember? Because he, John Doe, and not Cutler was the strong, demonic, and ag-gressive one."

"I really don't know what on earth you're talking about," Kati said.

"I should have known, sensed it, but no, I spend two days looking for evidence. Well, that's over. Perhaps we'll never find him, and certainly, we can never con-vict him. But we shall see."

He pulled on his trousers and said to Kati, "I dislike going there. The last time I was there, I came as a kins-man and left as a policeman."

"Be natural. When you are natural, you are the most charming man in the world."

"Ah, so. Yes. I will try. Don't wait up for me. I will probably be very late."

In spite of Masuto's apprehensions, Ishido appeared delighted to see him. He did Masuto the honor of answering the door himself, a small, smiling man in a magnificent black robe. Seated in Ishido's living room, which was tastefully but sparsely furnished in the Japanese manner, Masuto accepted a paper-thin teacup from an attractive young woman in her mid-twenties. The tea was green and pungent, and after it had been poured the attractive young woman disappeared. Well, Ishido was a widower. He was entitled to live as he saw fit.

"In the past, Masao," Ishido said to him, "you attempted a discussion in Japanese. Perhaps that was unfortunate."

"We will talk in English if you prefer," Masuto said.

"It will be better. It is the tongue you were born to and the tongue I have spoken for thirty-four years. There is a legend around, Masao, that I long for the old days. Nonsense! I love Los Angeles, and I shall die here. For a Buddhist, there is no foreign land."

"I must agree with you."

"You still meditate?" Ishido asked.

"Ah, yes. Indeed."

"Good. And Kati and the children?"

"All well."

"Good. Very good. Now what may I do for you, Masao? You have come with a rolled drawing in your hand. Do you desire my opinion as an art expert?"

Masuto unrolled the sketch the police artist had made and spread it out on the low tea table.

"I will not give you my opinion as an art expert," Ishido said.

"The work of a police artist. He draws well, if mechanically."

"Of course. So very sorry for my levity. For that purpose it is excellent."

"Tell me, sir," Masuto said, "is it true what I have heard?"

"And what have you heard?" Ishido asked, smiling.

"I must go beyond common courtesy, but it is absolutely necessary if you are to help me."

"A situation not uncommon."

"I have heard that you are as wealthy as Norton Simon, with better taste and a wider circle of influence here in southern California."

"I have never counted Norton's wealth, but I have the most profound respect for his taste. Are you after him?"

"Oh, no. Certainly not." Masuto pointed to the police drawing. "Do you know this man?"

Ishido studied the picture thoughtfully. "I'm afraid not. No, I have never seen that face before. Do you know him, Masao?"

Masuto took a long, deep breath. "Yes, as a skeleton we found under a swimming pool in Laurel Way."

"Ah, so. Yes. I read about the skeleton. Who murdered the man, Masao?"

"I hope that before I leave here tonight, honored kinsman, you will tell me his name. Otherwise . . ." Masuto folded his hands and shook his head.

"Am I a suspect, nephew?" Ishido asked undisturbed.

"Heaven forbid. Our suspect is five feet eight and a

half inches tall, and he weights at least fifty pounds more than you do."

"Remarkable, Masao. You know how tall he is and you know how heavy he is. Do you also know the color of his eyes?"

"Blue, I'm quite certain."

"Ah, so! We have here a game in the old sense, when they used to say that the only game worth anything was one where a human life was at stake. You have made a presumption that this man is a part of what the younger folk would call the southern California establishment."

"With all due humility, yes. And I am told that you know them all."

"Perhaps most, Masao. But satisfy my curiosity. Where did you get a picture of the man you found under the pool?"

"From the F.B.I. Except that I, being a fool, decided that this man is the murderer."

"But he is not."

"No, he is the victim."

"You pique my curiosity and my sense of the game. Let us discuss the murderer. He is five feet eight and a half, blue eyes, heavily built—and wealthy? But of course he would be wealthy if you place him in the establishment."

"In nineteen fifty," Masuto said, "he embezzled two million eight hundred thousand dollars from a bank. The embezzlement was not done by the murderer, but by his partner, whom he subsequently killed. I suspect he transferred the wealth to Los Angeles."

"Bearer bonds, some bank accounts," Ishido guessed.

"Ah, so," Masuto nodded. "But he is filled with a sense of power, aggressiveness. He must move into the community of power."

"The business world?"

"So I would guess."

Ishido poured some hot tea and sipped it. Then he closed his eyes and touched his fingers to his forehead. "Nineteen fifty-one—the latter half?"

"I can only guess, and I am reaching a point where I must doubt my guesses. The man under the pool was killed, I believe, in June or July of nineteen fifty. If it took him a year to establish himself—?"

"In what field?" Ishido asked mildly.

"I don't know. I have given no thought to that."

Smiling thinly, Ishido nodded. "Did I hear or read somewhere that these two people, the Lundmans, were killed with the bare hands of the murderer?"

"Perhaps I mentioned it. I am not sure it was in the papers."

"Karate?"

"I think so."

"So we add to our portrait, Masao. He is an enthusiast of the old art, which he perverts. To kill in karate is not only ignoble, but a perversion of all the excellence that endows the martial arts. Do you still practice, Masao?"

"Yes, when I can."

"Masao," Ishido said softly, "what hornets' nest do you stir up here? Tell me, do you have any evidence you can bring against this man?"

"No."

"So it is when you function in a democracy. Your police are very efficient, and at times, as for example with yourself, quite intelligent. But powerless. Here is a man who killed in cold blood—how many times did you say, Masao?"

"Six that I know of."

"Each killing predetermined, planned, executed with assassinlike precision, and we know of the murders and we know who he is. But we cannot touch him."

"Respected uncle!" Masuto said sharply.

"Yes?"

"You said we know who he is. True, we know who Stanley Cutler is. But I strongly suspect that Stanley Cutler is not the killer but instead is the victim."

"Ah, so. I agree."

"Then if you know who the killer is, you know who John Doe is."

"Yes. I think so. Insofar as knowledge and truth have any meaning or substance. Frequently I doubt that they do."

"Speaking philosophically, I agree with you. But in wholly mundane terms, uncle, do you know this man I seek?"

"I know one who fits your description. In nineteen fifty he bought a half interest in a small aerospace company in Orange County. I know him because we have had various business dealings and because we belong to the same country club, the West Los Angeles Club."

Amazed that his uncle, still Japanese for all his wealth and power and taste, had been admitted to the West Los Angeles Club, which had built such solid ramparts against Jews, Mexicans, and other lesser breeds, Masuto attempted to conceal his response; but Ishido simply shrugged and asked him, "Why so astonished, Masao?"

"Not at all."

"Come, come. You are absolutely amazed that they would admit me, a former officer in the imperial army, a Japanese, an Oriental, into their sacred precincts. But

133

my dear Masao, I am inordinately wealthy—which is all that counts. Then my having been with the army of the enemy becomes romantic, being an Oriental becomes exotic, and my being rather small and withered is overlooked—and in any case, my manners are so much better than theirs. So, you see, I was invited to join. I don't play golf, but I do frequently dine there, both for lunch and for dinner. The food is excellent. Ah, now!" He clapped his hands and grinned at Masuto. "We shall all dine there together, myself, you, and the murderer."

"You can't be serious?"

"But of course I am. Not only serious but enchanted. Can you guess who this man is who fits your description? Come, Masao, I have given you one hint already—the aerospace company. Let me give you another—the gift of twelve magnificent Picassos to the Los Angeles Museum of Art."

"Incredible," Masuto whispered. "It can't be. Saunders Aerospace is the largest company of its kind in the West. It's a prime supplier for the Pentagon. And Eric Saunders—you do mean Eric Saunders?"

"I certainly do," Ishido said cheerfully.

"You mean Eric Saunders is either Stanley Cutler or—"

Ishido poured another cup of tea and handed it to Masuto. "Come now, nephew. It is time to end this confusion. You showed me that very clever drawing of Stanley Cutler as he would be today if he were made over by a plastic surgeon. There is no Stanley Cutler. The skeleton is Stanley Cutler. Eric Saunders is Eric Saunders, very clean, as they say here, very public. No secrets in Eric Saunders's past, no need for plastic surgery or any of that nonsense. We are talking about one of a half dozen of the most distinguished citizens of southern California, an industrial tycoon of major national importance. He is the youngest son of the Earl of Newton. You know, Masao, when the old Earl died and the estate was neck deep in debt, Eric bought it and made a gift of it to the British National Trust. Didn't want it himself. He's an American citizen, member of the Republican National Committee, president of Saunders Aerospace, on a dozen boards, including several fine universities, a millionaire a hundred times over, and a member of the West Los Angeles Country Club."

"And also a murderer?"

"Who knows? But what an incredible possibility! You know, he does fit your description. Came here in nineteen fifty or so with apparently unlimited funds. People took it for granted that he had a line of credit from his British bankers. But he might well have laundered the money through Mexico and back to England and then here. He's about the height you want, blue eyes, fifty-nine or sixty, I would say, splendid physical condition."

"Is he a friend of yours?" Masuto asked.

"Ah, that would be an unhappy turn of events. No. Neither a friend nor an enemy, although I should not enjoy having him as an enemy. But if he is the man you seek, he is certainly not your common murderer."

"In some ways, yes," Masuto said. "He is as much a psychopath as any downtown hoodlum. In other ways—well, he presents problems."

"You must meet him of course?"

"Why should he care to meet me?" Masuto wondered.

"I will tell him that you are a master of the true Okinawan art."

"Karate? He practices karate?"

"Of course."

"Then he is my man," Masuto said, nodding somberly.

"No, nephew. You have no evidence. He is possibly a murderer, but not your man. No one's man."

The young woman appeared again, bearing a fresh pot of tea. She wore a black silk kimono, embroidered in gold thread. She set down the teapot and left. Ishido poured the tea, and then looked inquiringly at Masuto.

"Something troubles you?" Ishido asked, a note of mockery in his voice.

"Why do you give him to me?"

"Ah. Isn't it my duty to aid the police?"

"With all due respect, I cannot accept such an explanation."

"Then let us simply say that my karma involves Saunders. You are a Buddhist. You comprehend karma."

"How long have you known Saunders? You said he came here in nineteen fifty. Did you meet him then?"

Ishido smiled. "You are very clever, Masao, but you are also very presumptuous. I think we have talked enough. If you wish to know more about my relationship with Eric Saunders and why I lead you to him, join us for dinner as I suggested."

A few minutes later Masuto left Ishido's house, aware that he was being used and irritated because he had no notion of why and how he was being used.

12
THE BOMB

The following morning, which was Thursday, Ishido telephoned Masuto at home. Kati answered the phone, and the fact that it was Ishido placed her in a quandary. For one thing Ishido was the most romantic and unapproachable part of her life. He was wealthy beyond Kati's imagination; women had threaded in and out of his life; and he would embark for Tokyo as casually as Kati might embark for the closest supermarket. On the other hand, Masuto was meditating when Ishido called, and Kati fiercely resisted interrupting him at his meditation.

"He will return your call in a few minutes, honored uncle. A thousand apologies."

"A thousand apologies are too many, my darling," Masuto told her a while later. "Your kinsman, Ishido, is both a hunter and a game player. Like all men of great wealth, his life is a struggle against boredom, and I have displaced his boredom with a new and fascinating game. Believe me, he will find me. I cannot evade him until he sees this new game played out."

"I don't understand—"

The telephone rang.

"Ah, so! Unless I miss my guess, there is Ishido again."

Kati anwered the phone and then handed it to her husband. "It is my honorable uncle."

"I must apologize," Masuto told Ishido. "I was at my meditation."

"Of course. How insufferable of me to interrupt it. And now?"

"Now I am finished."

"Ah, so. Very good." Ishido, for all of his imperturbability, could not keep the excitement out of his voice. "I have spoken to my old acquaintance, Eric Saunders, and in spite of the fact that he has one of the most active social and business schedules of perhaps any man in southern California, he will be delighted to dine with both of us at the club tonight."

"Why?" Masuto asked coldly.

If Ishido caught the icy note in Masuto's voice, he gave no sign of it, simply repeating, "This evening at my club, Masao."

"I asked you why? Why should a man of affairs and of his importance take the time to dine with an ordinary policeman?"

"Perhaps because he understands that you are not an ordinary policeman. Perhaps because I mentioned your consuming interest in the skeleton that was discovered under the swimming pool."

"No, that's not enough. You are using me," Masuto said angrily.

"And were you not willing to use me? Of course I am using you, and you in turn are using me. This is no common homicide, Masao. You are up against a titan."

"No, sir, if you will forgive me. I am up against a sick and vile man, a psychopath, someone who should be locked up before he does more hurt to more people."

"As you will."

"Why did he agree to dine with us?"

"Because I told him you had discovered that the skeleton under the pool was that of a man named Stanley Cutler."

"I see. And how did he react to that?"

"At first there was no reaction at all. Then he looked at me with a sort of malignant curiosity. Oh, yes, Masao, he would not hesitate to kill me should the occasion arise. Of course, I am not one of those who is easily killed, and perhaps he understands that. You see, he does respect me, or he would not have seen me so late at night and on such short notice. Yes, he agreed to dine with us."

"What is the source of your own hatred?" Masuto asked.

"My hatred?"

"Yes, your hatred."

"You press me back too many years, Masao. You are born in this country and you are not yet forty years old. Let me say only that our paths crossed in Burma many years ago, and this man, Eric Saunders, shot a Japanese prisoner in cold blood. Such things were done by both sides, but Saunders—well, I waited, and my patience was rewarded."

"There is no evidence that will convict him," Masuto said angrily. "You know that as well as I do."

"You will manage, nephew. I have faith in you."

When he put down the telephone, Kati mentioned his irritation. "What has Ishido done to annoy you so?"

"He has put me in an impossible position."

"I am sorry."

"It will be all right," Masuto assured her as he kissed her and then left the house. But would it be—and in what way? He found himself looking over his shoulder, and before he started his car, he looked underneath it and then under the hood. The threat of Eric Saunders was not simply the threat of a single man, but the threat of great amounts of money and of vast resources. Masuto knew that there was no protection against assassination, no protection against a determined killer. He might miss once, twice, three times—but in the end he would be successful. Well, perhaps Ishido was right to drive the thing to its end, whatever the end might be.

Instead of going directly to the police station, Masuto stopped off at the Beverly Hills office of Merrill Lynch, Pierce, Fenner & Smith, where his cousin, Alan Toyada, was in charge of research.

"No, don't tell me," Toyada greeted him. "They have raised your wages. You have money to invest. You're on the take now—"

"Your humor is puerile and infantile."

"It's not my humor, Masao. You're always so damn bloody serious."

"Unfortunately, I live in that world."

"Forgive the humor. What can I do for you?"

"Eric Saunders."

"Ah. And from what point of view?"

"To begin, an investment."

"For yourself? I mean—well, who knows, it is possible that Ishido passed on suddenly. Supposedly, he has no children, but from what I have heard, his heirs might well pop up all over the place. On the other hand, Kati would, I am sure, come in for a large piece of capital which should be properly invested."

"I come to you as a policeman, not as an investor," Masuto said, and possibly would have added that unless Toyada stopped babbling, nothing would be accomplished—except that Toyada was thin-skinned, as well as insensitive, a more common combination than one might suppose.

"Oh, yes, of course, Masao. But you asked me about Saunders as an investment."

"I'm curious."

"Excellent, excellent. Profits have gone up at least fifteen percent a year for five years now. Amazing record. The stock has doubled during the past twelve months."

"How do you account for that?"

"Good engineers. Space contracts. And of course their new shuttle passenger plane. They have almost a billion dollars in back orders. It's a short-haul shuttle, lands anywhere, carries two hundred and forty passengers, wide body, comfortable. Oh, yes, if I had the money, I'd buy."

"And how much of this is due to Saunders himself?"

"That's hard to say. He still plays an active role in

the company, makes the hard decisions, but I hear he has his fingers in other pies as well—museums, films, politics."

"What are his politics?"

"Well, he does government work, so he's for the administration, but they say he plays both sides of the fence. I imagine he does."

"And what about his morality?" Masuto asked.

"I don't think you mean women, Masao?"

"No, I don't mean women."

"Well, you know as well as I do that you can't discuss big business in terms of morality. Rules, yes, morality, no."

"All right, Alan, rules. Does he break the rules?"

"No more than anyone else. I'm sure he pays off wherever it's necessary, but who doesn't? He doesn't raid other companies, but then he doesn't have to. He's his own steamroller and he's driving Saunders Aerospace right to the top."

"Has he ever married?"

"No, which doesn't mean he's gay. He's had a parade of women through his life."

"How does that come into your financial research?" Masuto asked curiously.

"It doesn't. I read *Los Angeles* magazine and a few of its lesser companion journals. He's mentioned frequently. Tell me, why all this interest? What do you know that I don't know, now that you've squeezed all that I do know out of me?"

"Nothing that would be helpful."

"Have you got something on Saunders? Are you going to bust him? Should we go short on the stock?"

"No way I know of that I can bust him," Masuto said.

"If you do, give me an edge."

"I promise," Masuto said.

Back at the station house, Masuto told Wainwright about his talk with Ishido and Ishido's conclusions.

"You ask me," Wainwright said, "your Uncle Ishido is leaping to some pretty dangerous and far out conclusions. Eric Saunders is not nobody. He's one of the most prominent citizens in our town, nationally known, a man of wealth and power. If one word of our discussion were to leak out of here, Masao, he could sue us right off the face of the map. And he would too. What in hell makes this Ishido so sure of himself?"

"Ishido is hard to explain. You know that he was in the old imperial army. He will never return to Japan, but he also never forgets that he is Japanese. There is some indication upon Ishido's part that he crossed paths with Saunders somewhere in the East, perhaps in Burma, and that he had a grudge against Saunders."

"Which would certainly not promote any objectivity on his part."

"Except for one thing, which worries me and complicates this even further. Last night Ishido either telephoned Saunders or saw him in person. Ishido told him that I knew the man under the pool was Stanley Cutler and that I also knew that Saunders had killed him. You see, tonight, Saunders, Ishido, and I will dine together at Ishido's club, and I can think of no reason on earth why Saunders should have agreed to this dinner unless Ishido told him what I knew."

"What in hell does Ishido think he's up to?"

143

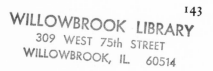

"He's playing a game."

"And where do we come in?"

"I don't know," Masuto said slowly.

"But since Saunders agreed, you feel there's no question but that he's our man?"

"None."

"So to come back to the skeleton under the pool, the reason why there was never a report of someone missing is very simple. There never was anyone missing except Cutler, and everyone concluded that he had taken off. Saunders never had to hide. He took the money, laundered it, and appeared on the scene here as a young British millionaire. And there is not a damn thing we can do about it. Then why does he want to meet you?"

"I suppose it's a conceit. He knows we can't touch him, and a dangerous game is nothing new to him. Then there's still our only ace in the hole—Rosita. I think he would like to know something about me. He is black belt karate and probably versed in all of the martial arts. Very often, Westerners who take up the martial art make a kind of pseudo-religion out of it—and I'm sure Ishido told him I have some skill in karate."

"Come off that," Wainwright said harshly. "No games!"

"The games are there."

"If you are thinking of fighting Saunders in this goddamn Chinese wrestling art of yours, forget it."

"Will he forget it?"

"You know, Masao, there's one thing you damn well better get used to. Criminals go free. Some crimes are punished; a hell of a lot of them are not. There is no way, no way in the world that you could charge Saunders and make it stick. Quite to the contrary, he may be sitting with his lawyers right this minute ready to sue the city for all we've got."

"Not really," Masuto said. "There isn't enough money on earth to make Saunders put himself on a witness stand or put me on a witness stand. We can't do anything, neither can he. It's a standoff."

"You know I got to give this to the L.A. cops and to the Inglewood cops," Wainwright said.

"Why?"

"It's procedure. You know that, Masao."

"Suppose they make waves? Suppose they decide to question Saunders?"

"That's their privilege."

"Would it hurt to hold off a day or two?"

"Would it help?"

"Maybe," Masuto said. "Nothing about this case becomes simpler, only more and more complicated. We were sure that Stanley Cutler had murdered the man under the swimming pool. Then the man under the swimming pool became Stanley Cutler, and the killer is someone called Eric Saunders whom neither of us has ever met. Let me take it one step further—"

But Matuso did not take it one step further. The telephone rang. It was Sy Beckman at the hotel, and he said quietly, "Masao, I think both doors into the corridor, Rosita's and mine, are booby-trapped. I heard some sounds, and I hiked myself up to where I could look over the transom. There's a steel box sitting in front of each door, and from the look of it, they're ratchet loaded.

I alerted Gellman to keep the help away from the two doors. I thought maybe you and Wainwright should get the L.A.P.D. bomb squad over here and get here yourselves, because I'll be damned if I know what to do."

"Is there no way out except through the doors?"

"We're up three floors, Masao. If those charges are big enough, the whole wing could go. We're over the pool and the gardens, so you couldn't even get a fire truck under these windows. It's a hell of a situation, and if we ever get out of this, I'm going to get Wainwright to slap them with every violation under the sun."

"Meanwhile, I want you out of there. Make a rope of bedsheets, bedspreads, and blankets and lower Rosita to the ground, and then you slide down yourself. Now. Right now! We'll be there in ten minutes."

Then Masuto called the hotel and spoke to Gellman. "Oh, it's great," Gellman said. "You've really done it, sergeant. Just a couple of rooms for a few days, and now I got to explain to the board how come half the hotel was blown away."

"They haven't blown anything yet," Masuto said soothingly. "Just empty that wing and don't touch the booby traps. That will keep you from facing lawsuits."

"Beautiful. Now you're protecting me."

"I'm trying to."

"What's going on?" Wainwright demanded.

"Just let me call the bomb squad and I'll explain."

Driving to the Beverly Glen Hotel at top speed, Masuto said, "He uses us, manipulates us, controls us. He got her out of the room. That was all he wanted, but what could I do? What could I do? I couldn't leave them in there and let both of them die."

"For Christ's sake, Masao, nobody's died yet."

That was not so. Rosita was dead by the time Masuto or the ambulance reached the hotel. She had been shot three times while Beckman was lowering her from the window, once in the head and twice in the body.

13

ERIC SAUNDERS

As if she were his own daughter, he hid his face to hide his tears. It was not his style to weep over the dead. He observed the routine; the routine was a necessity. Half a mile away were high rise apartments, and within half an hour, the rifle, a beautifully crafted Mauser-type five shot, was found on the rooftop of one of the apartment houses. The rifle was identified by the L.A.P.D. gun expert as a small-shop product, probably made in Italy or France about twenty years before. Masuto was uninterested. Police channels and thoroughness were not made for criminals of this type. Eventually, they would find out who made the gun, who sold it, who bought it, and it would all lead nowhere.

Beckman said, "My God, Masao, I never thought of it. It never occurred to me."

"I know."

"I figured those damn bombs were going off any

moment, and then after I spoke to you, all I wanted was to get her out of there. She was a lovely kid. I was falling in love with that kid."

"I know."

"Masao, just let me get my hands on the bastard who did it—"

The bomb men didn't want anyone in the hallway where they were working, but Masuto insisted and pushed past the guards.

"Sergeant, it's off limits, even to you."

Beckman followed him, as if one could not do penance apart from the other. Stevenson, from the bomb squad, who knew Masuto, explained what they were up against. "Beckman guessed right. It's ratchet and spring. The contraption is attached with suction cups; it's wound in and then when it's flat up against the surface—in this case the door—the pawl latches on the fuse. The slightest movement blows it, and no way to get into it. It's simple, foolproof, and deadly, and so help me God, Masuto, I don't know how to handle this one."

"Unless, of course, there's no explosive in the metal box."

"I don't go in for such guesses. When I see a bomb, I function on the theory that it's loaded. This one has a clock mechanism as well as the ratchet and pawl. We'll have to empty the hotel."

"He had his marksman waiting half a mile away on a rooftop. The only function of that damn box was to get the girl out of the window."

"I can't take the chance."

"The hell with it!" Masuto said. "Come on, Sy, let's get out of here."

In the lobby downstairs Gellman stopped Masuto,

pleading, "My God, sergeant, what are you doing to me? They're emptying the hotel, and half of it may be blown to kingdom come. You try to be a good guy, and this is how it ends."

"It won't be blown away," Masuto said tiredly. "I don't know what else to tell you. I'm sorry this had to happen. The girl is dead, so she's got the real short end."

They left the hotel and Beckman said he needed a drink, and Masuto suggested a quiet place in Culver City, where they could sit and talk. Beckman had two double scotches and Masuto drank beer. "I don't know," Beckman said, "day and night together—I never met anyone like that kid, just a Mexican girl and an illegal, but the sweetest, kindest kid in the world."

"Revenge is no good," Masuto told him. "It solves nothing, satisfies nothing."

"Goddamn you, Masao, you know who did it!"

"Yes."

"I want him!"

"We all do. We're not avenging angels. We're not terrorists who make our own justice, and we're not juries. We're cops."

"What are you telling me—that we can't touch him?"

"No, we'll touch him, even without Rosita. It's not touching him—it's trying to make some sense out of this, because right now it makes no damn sense at all." He went to the telephone and called the Beverly Glen Hotel and asked for the desk. "This is Sergeant Masuto. What's the situation with the bombs?"

"Duds, sir. They went off a few minutes ago. A couple of firecrackers in each one. No damage to speak of."

Masuto walked back to the table where Beckman was working at the problem of getting drunk. "Go home,

Sy," Masuto told him. "Go home and finish a bottle and sleep it off."

"What for? I got a lousy marriage. Home—home is to laugh, Masao. I'm not so old. I'm not forty yet. I could have married that Mexican kid and had everything I ever dreamed of having."

"The only world is right here," Masuto told him, putting an arm around the big man. "Come on, Sy, I'm going to drive you home."

"What about Wainwright?"

"I'll talk to him."

Masuto dropped Beckman off at his home, and then he drove back to the station and told Wainwright that Beckman was drunk and sleeping it off.

"What in hell do you mean, drunk—it's two o'clock in the afternoon!"

"I encouraged him. That Mexican kid meant a great deal to him. Stop pushing us. We're both human."

"Well, don't get your ass up. Who's pushing who?"

"Sorry, so sorry. I want this to be over."

"I told you to leave it alone and let it be over."

"Not that way."

"You think Saunders shot the kid?"

"Himself? No," Masuto said. "Did he hire the gun? A few hours ago I would have said yes, without any question. Now I don't know."

"You don't want to talk about it?"

"Tomorrow."

"You're still going to see Saunders tonight?"

"Oh, yes. That I would not miss for anything."

"Be careful, Masao."

But no, Masuto told himself as he drove away from the police station. He was not threatened, nor was he in the line of fire—unless—no, that must be expelled from his mind. He must clear his mind and know exactly what he would say to his uncle, Naga Orashi. That was Monday when he had seen Naga; what was today? Wednesday? No, Wednesday was the day with the police artist. Today is Thursday, and the whole thing began only six days ago, when the heavy rains under-mined a swimming pool and sent it sliding down into a canyon. And since then four more people had died.

He drove into the yard of Naga's construction com-pany, and there was his wife's uncle Naga, sitting in his rocking chair, as if only a few minutes had gone by since Masuto had last seen him, nibbling at cold tea rice, caked and threaded through with ginger.

"Have some," he said to Masuto.

"Thank you. I am most grateful and very hungry, since I missed my lunch somewhere during the day."

"So? Indeed? So very busy, yet you find time to come and chat with this old Japanese gentleman."

"Why didn't you tell me that Ishido operated a back-hoe?"

Naga stared at Masuto for a long moment, and then he shook his head sadly. "Granted that you were born in this country, and granted that your Japanese is abomi-nable, and granted that you have absorbed barbarian habits—granting all this, one would imagine that you still retain some comprehension of the fitness of things."

"We are not speaking of the fitness of things. We speak about the fact that I came to you as a policeman and you saw no reason to tell me that Ishido operated a backhoe."

"Perhaps you should not have come as a policeman, Masao."

ERIC SAUNDERS

"Oh?"

"Think about it. I am Kati's mother's brother. How would you characterize us in old Japan? Shopkeepers, perhaps. Ishido is tied by a marriage to Kati's father, so she is not of his blood. Ishido is of seven generations of Samurai. His father was an advisor to the old emperor. When Ishido was twenty-five years old, he was a colonel in the imperial army. He was decorated, honored; and when finally Japan fell, he could not remain there, shamed, dishonored. You would not understand why he came here; it's an old form, the vanquished honoring the victor—a very old and honorable Japanese gesture, but one that evoked nothing from the conqueror who couldn't care less whether this young Japanese Samurai starved to death or not. Whereupon, I gave Ishido a job."

"And he learned to operate a backhoe?"

"Nephew, I did not conceal this from you. You never asked me, and it was so many years ago that the circumstances are most vague in my mind."

"But he did operate a backhoe?"

"Yes, as I recall. It was an opportunity for him to earn a bit more. Only for a while. Ishido was very clever."

"And did you perhaps rent this backhoe, driver and all, to Alex Brody when he built the house on Laurel Way?"

The old man knit his brows. "I don't know. Did I rent it or just lend it for a few days? It was so long ago."

"And Ishido with it? Come, dear uncle, try to remember."

"Possibly."

"You should have told me."

"You are chasing ghosts, Masao. The past is dead. We

153

who are Japanese should know that better than others. How could we live if the past were not dead?"

"I am not Japanese," Masuto said unhappily. "I was born here in California. My wife was born here, and my children here."

"No, you are not Japanese," Naga agreed. "But in a manner of speaking, Ishido is your kinsman."

"I'll be back in a moment," Masuto said. He walked to his car, and from the trunk rack, he took the photocopy that the F.B.I. had sent to him. He brought it to Naga.

"You know this man?" he asked Naga.

"A thing like this," Naga said, blinking at the photocopy, "it could be anyone. It was so long ago—"

"Or someone."

"How did you come by this picture, Masao?"

Masao shook his head. "I can't explain that now. But when I leave, honored uncle, there is no need to telephone Ishido and warn him. He knows what I know."

"I have not spoken to Ishido in more than twenty years," Naga said sadly. "I have no love or affection for him. But we are kinsmen. Of course, I am speaking out of a lack of knowledge. Mr. Lundman and his wife were killed, a terrible thing. Ishido did not do that."

"And the skeleton under the swimming pool?"

"Who knows what went on there? Who will ever know?"

"You told me the grave could not be dug with a backhoe. It is your business to know such things. Now I must ask you again—could the grave have been dug with a backhoe?"

Still studying the photo and without looking up, Naga said, "This is a very strange picture indeed, Masao, not of any person, but—" He switched into Japanese. "A thing lurks in shadow and asks for recognition." And then in English, "Is it not an article of your Buddhist thinking that the vibrations of the subject are in the drawing?"

"It is an article of damn nonsense!" Masuto said with irritation. "I asked you a simple question. Should I go elsewhere? There are twenty contractors in this city whom I can ask to join me on Laurel Way, and who will give me a plain answer as to whether that grave was dug with a backhoe."

"Gently, gently, Masao," the old man begged him. "Why such anger?"

"Because murder angers me."

"All right. Listen then. Your twenty contractors could not give you a firm answer. If your backhoe had a ten-inch claw spread, then it could have gouged out the grave and made the final shaping easier."

"Why didn't you tell me that the other day?"

"You know why."

"And what do you find there?" Masuto asked harshly, pointing to the photo.

"A resemblance."

"To whom?"

"To a laborer, I think. It was long ago."

"What? Or to Eric Saunders?"

"Not obviously. If I saw it somewhere, in a book or a newspaper, I would not think of Mr. Saunders."

"But you do think of him now?"

"I don't know—"

"Perhaps you have been thinking a great deal about Mr. Saunders?"

"Masao, Masao, we shelter our kinsmen when we can. I would do it for you. You would do it for me."

"Uncle," Masuto said with annoyance, "what kind of talk is that? Shelter a kinsman when he is hungry or cold, but a murderer?" He stalked over to the car, and this time he returned with the drawing the police artist had made under Dr. Hartman's direction. "And this?" he demanded, thrusting the drawing at Naga. "This is not so long ago that your memory must fail you."

"Am I a criminal that you speak to me so?" Naga asked unhappily.

"You are my revered uncle. But you must tell me the truth."

"Yes, it's Saunders. He had his face changed. I knew and Ishido knew—"

"Do you also know you are in terrible danger?"

"I am an old man. Each night I go to sleep with the knowledge that I may not awaken. I am not afraid of danger."

For a long moment, Masuto studied his uncle. Then he asked, more gently, "What dealings did Ishido have with Eric Saunders?"

"I know very little of what went on there. I don't even know how they met. I only remember that Saunders needed someone who could speak Japanese. There was a litigation of a landholding in the San Fernando Valley, land that had belonged to Japanese nationals and was seized by the government. I think it comprised eleven hundred acres. Saunders bought the land at auction, and then Ishido joined him to fight the litigation that the Japanese nationals brought against them. Eventually, they settled, and Ishido's share was almost half a million dollars. That was the beginning of his fortune."

"And the beginning of Mr. Saunders's fortune?"

"No, he was already wealthy. The story was that he

was a sort of cast-off son of an important British family."
The old man blinked his eyes and then stared at Masuto
unhappily. "Of course, the story is a lie."

"Yes."

"And what happened at the hotel today?"

"How do you know about that?"

"As with all things today, Masao, it was on the air
immediately. Is it connected?"

"Yes."

The old man hesitated, then he said, "Be very careful,
Masao."

"I always am."

"Don't think of yourself as a kinsman. I assure you,
they have stopped thinking of you in that fashion."

"They? Why do you say they?"

The old man shrugged.

"Is there bad blood between Ishido and Saunders?"

"Why should there be?"

"I asked you."

"Ah, so, of course. I would think not. From what my
sons tell me, Saunders made it possible for Ishido to
belong to the West Los Angeles Country Club. It is not
a thing that pleases me, to see a member of the old
aristocracy using influence to belong to a club where
the only qualification for membership is to have money
and to be neither Jewish nor Oriental nor black nor
Mexican. I myself would have no part of such a place,
but it was something Ishido desired."

"But you say that he and Saunders have remained
close all these years?"

"So I am told, so my sons tell me. In fact, I have heard
that currently Ishido is engaged in negotiations with
Tokyo Airlines for the purchase of some sixteen Saunders

airbuses at a price of twenty-eight million dollars each—
that is, acting for Saunders."

"I feel like Alice in Wonderland," Masuto said.

"Oh?"

"A children's book."

"Have I done something very wrong, Masao?"

"No—no, I think not, uncle."

14

THE GAME
PLAYERS

Kati knew and understood Masuto better than he
imagined. She understood the strange psychology opera-
tive in a man who earns twenty thousand dollars a year
to protect those who make two hundred thousand and
even two million. Being a policeman in Beverly Hills is
certainly somewhat different from being a policeman
anywhere else, and being a Nisei only complicates it
further. Yet Masuto was not judgmental. He had neither
contempt for wealth nor admiration for wealth. As an
abstraction, he saw neither virtue nor evil in wealth; it
was simply a fact of the society he worked in. Yet tonight, as he dressed himself in a clean white shirt, gray
flannel trousers, and his best blue blazer—indeed his only
blue blazer—Kati noticed that he appeared even more
unhappy than the approaching evening should have
caused him to be. She watched him toy with his gun,
trying to make the shoulder holster unnoticeable under

the well-fitted jacket. The jacket was too well fitted. When he stretched it to button, the gun bulged wickedly.

"Will you need the gun, Masao?" she asked gently. "Surely in the West Los Angeles Country Club an occasion to use a gun is not very likely. And anyone will know you have a gun there."

"Regulations—" Masuto sighed and put the gun aside. He selected a knitted black tie, thinking that he, like Ishido, was still a victim of the old ways. In all truth, he did not want the gun. The game precluded it.

"Masao, with a white shirt—you have nicer ties. This striped tie I gave you for your birthday and which you have never worn, well, it is much nicer than a black tie. You're not going to a funeral."

"No?"

"I haven't seen Ishido for years, but I do remember how charming and bright he is. It should be an absolutely delightful evening, if you would only relax and allow yourself to enjoy it. Who did you say the other man was?"

"Eric Saunders."

"I don't mind a bit. It's very old country, three men having dinner with no women, except geisha girls." Kati giggled. "In the West Los Angeles Country Club, geishas. Can you imagine?"

"Not very well, no."

"Oh, Masao, you are so somber." Kati was tying the striped tie now. "No one ever takes me to such a place. If they did, I would be quite happy about it." She tightened the tie fold. "There. That looks elegant. Have you ever been to the club before?"

"It's not a place I frequent."

"Then you must tell me all about it."

Not all of it, certainly, Masuto thought. Not the way the car jockey at the club looked at his old Datsun. Masuto had forgone the small conceit of using his police identification card, and in any case, it would have been out of place there and would have attracted attention to himself. He simply drove up to the door, taking his place in the line of Rolls-Royces, Mercedes, Jaguars, Lincolns, and Cadillacs. If one can conceive of a car held at arm's length, slightly off the ground, faced with pinched nostrils, then one can understand Masuto's irritation—which he fought, telling himself, This is not the time or place for irritation. Soon, the game begins. Stay cool and steady. Which was commendable advice, since he had been fool enough to leave his gun behind—a fact which he was beginning to regret a great deal.

Ishido was waiting for him in the lobby, and he welcomed Masuto with great cordiality. "Indeed, nephew, I had thought that perhaps you might not come."

"Why? When I face a killer, I have what I might call my moment of truth. They are few and far between."

"And you are convinced that Eric Saunders is your killer?"

"You convinced me, Ishido-san."

Ishido stared at him thoughtfully. Then he bowed slightly. "Come and meet him, Masao."

Masuto followed Ishido into the dining room, a charming room done in the Spanish colonial style, the floor and walls tiled, a handsome fireplace at one end.

The headwaiter recognized Ishido, expressed pleasure at seeing him, and led him and Masuto to a table in one corner of the room. The man already seated at this table rose as they appeared and welcomed Masuto warmly. "I have heard much about you," he said.

"And I about you, Mr. Saunders."

They stood face-to-face for a moment, Masuto taller, leaner, younger—but also aware of the tremendous strength in the hand that gripped his. Saunders was built like a bull, the build of a man who is overmuscled but fights his weight successfully. For a man close to sixty, he appeared to be in marvelous physical condition, the skin tight around his face and neck, his stomach flat.

"Please, sit down," Saunders said. Masuto seated himself, Ishido on one side of him, Saunders on the other. The headwaiter was hovering over them. "I ordered champagne," Saunders said, and turned to Masuto. "You do drink champagne? Just a taste for each of us, a drink to whatever we drink to. I think we should drink lightly and eat lightly."

"For the sake of the game," Ishido said.

"Naturally," Saunders said.

When the champagne had been poured, Saunders raised his glass, but no one spoke a toast, or cheers, or anything of that kind.

"I hear from Ishido," Saunders said, "that you are a most unusual policeman. I would guess that you are studying my face with such intensity to see whether you can detect scar tissue or suture marks. But before we go any further, Masuto, I must ask whether you are wired?"

"And if I were, why should you imagine that I would tell you?"

"A sense of honor."

"Honor?" Masuto asked in amazement. "You really confront me with a thing called honor?"

"I speak of you," Saunders said. "Not of myself, not of Ishido. He tells me that you are a Zen Buddhist, that you practice meditation as well as the Okinawan art. If you tell me you are not wired, I believe you."

"I am not wired."

"I didn't think you were."

Masuto's mouth was dry. He sipped at the champagne. Actually, he did not care for champagne, and he had little desire to drink with these two men.

"I am not asking for truth," Masuto said. "To find truth between the two of you would be like seeking a lump of sugar in a pool of molasses. But you, Ishido, what advantage by lying to me?"

"Did he lie?" Saunders smiled. "Where does the truth end and a lie begin? Ishido said you very cleverly put together a picture of me, but that it did not resemble me at all."

"Then you are Stanley Cutler?"

"No, no, no, Masuto. What a dreadful mess you have made of everything. Thirty years, during which I live my life and Ishido lives his life, and then a rainstorm and a Nisei detective on a small-town police force destroy everything. I am not Stanley Cutler, Masuto, I am Eric Saunders. I was christened Eric Arthur Sutherland Saunders, and I am the youngest son of the Earl of Newton."

"Then it was Cutler's skeleton?"

Saunders laughed. "No, no, indeed."

"I think we should order dinner," Ishido said. "We will eat lightly, but we should eat and preserve the amenities. What would your pleasure be, Masao?"

"Whatever you wish."

"Surely you have a preference? Or is the company so unpleasant that you have no appetite?"

"The chicken, since you insist," Masuto said, thinking that they were both quite mad. But then, are not all murderers quite mad, and might not one say that this madness had become the condition of a great part of mankind? They chatted over the food, hardly eating, only toying with the meal. If they meant Masuto to feel the strain, they succeeded, and finally, unable to contain himself, he asked them flatly, "Which one of you killed Stanley Cutler?"

"Why? Why, Masao?" Ishido asked him. "Thirty years. What good comes of this?"

"Let me explain," Saunders said. "Since there is nothing you can ever do about it, since there is no way you can ever prosecute either of us, you should have your bone, the reward of the hunter. I would have rewarded you otherwise, but Ishido said no. Killing you would hardly be worth the price of Ishido's enmity."

"Hardly magnanimous," Masuto said. "You still plan to kill me."

"Who knows?"

"When dinner is over," Ishido said, "you may leave here, and no harm will come to you. You have my word."

"I am waiting for the explanation."

"I created Cutler," Saunders said. "He was killed in Burma. I was with him. I think I got the notion from his prints—or lack of them. Burned off in a flaming tank." He held out one hand. "Doesn't look much different, does it, but if you look closely, you'll find no recognizable prints. I turned myself into Cutler. Oh,

164

don't think it was easy—it took months of planning, years to carry it out."

"Cutler's body?"

"I took his dog tags and blew his head off with a grenade. You have no idea how much confusion war engenders. We were of a size and he had no family, so I had the pleasant choice of being one of two persons, whichever I preferred."

"You blew his head off with a grenade," Masuto said. "Was he alive then, or was he dead?"

"Always the policeman. You want another murder to add to your list? I'm afraid I can't oblige you. He was dead when I blew his head off. I got the job at Manhattan National Bank as Stanley Cutler." He paused and smiled. Ishido took a cigar, clipped the end, and lit it. "Odd to think of it. I never fancied working at a bank, but embezzlement is so enticingly easy. Of course today with the computers everywhere, it's even easier. When I finished the job and had soaked the money away here in Los Angeles as Eric Saunders, I simply put all that was Stanley Cutler, a few cards, one or two other things, down the toilet—flushed them away."

"Then who," Masuto asked, "was the skeleton under the pool?"

"Ah, yes—the source of all our unhappiness. You see, when I was very young, I did a bit of embezzlement, but awkwardly, on a London bank. I was caught and it was hushed up because of my family, and I went into the army. Then, when I did the job at the Midtown Manhattan Bank, this Scotland Yard chap who was in on the first screw-up, drew some conclusions, got himself a a leave of absence, and turned up in Los Angeles—not to arrest me, mind you, but to threaten me into a split.

Ishido happened to be with me that night. I had spotted some acreage in the San Fernando Valley and I needed a Japanese partner for the deal. The C.I.D. man was foolish enough to turn his back on me, and then there was the problem of what to do with the body. This one did have fingerprints, and I had to make sure that he vanished for good. Ishido was operating a backhoe on a job, and he suggested putting the body under the swimming pool. Well, once it turned up—there it was, with two people in L.A. who could put Ishido on that job and point a finger at both of us."

"Two people?" Masuto asked.

"The old lady and Lundman. Lundman's wife happened to be there. So it was with the Mexican girl."

"Who never saw you," Masuto said bitterly. "You damned, murderous bastard—Naga Orashi, the contractor, was the man who hired Ishido to drive the backhoe, and he's alive!"

Saunders looked coldly at Ishido, who shrugged and said, "He is my kinsman. I told you he was dead."

"You lied to me."

"I have various loyalties," Ishido said. "Don't try to understand them."

"It makes a debt you have to settle," Saunders said thinly. "You upset the apple cart."

"I changed the game slightly." Ishido shrugged.

"You know where it puts me."

"You do what you must do, Eric."

"Another kinsman?"

"Not exactly. As I said, you will do what you must do."

Listening to all this with increasing disgust, Masuto

interrupted harshly. "Do you know, gentlemen, I am going to arrest both of you. I know I don't have one scrap of evidence and that not one charge will stick, but I can parade this before the media in a way that will convince the public. They will try you, even if no jury can."

"So you came here," Saunders said, "to satisfy your curiosity and to make a public spectacle of us. I would have to be childish not to have anticipated that. Look behind you, Masuto."

Masuto turned. At the table behind him, two men were sitting. They both had long, hard, sallow faces, and when he glanced at them, they nodded coldly.

"A word from me, just a movement of my hand, and you will be dead, Masuto. Don't try to arrest us. I have other plans."

"Really? What other plans?"

Masuto glanced at Ishido. He had become passive. He sat with his hands folded—as if he had placed a hood over himself and between him and the two men.

"I am a devotee of karate, of the Okinawan style."

"No, you are despoiler of a way. You desecrate and debase a noble thing. Karate is not to kill."

"No? Then what is its purpose?"

"To defend, to bring some enlightenment to those who practice it with love and reverence. But you, Saunders, you have made it your own obscenity. You have taken something you don't understand, something beyond the understanding of men like yourself, and turned it into an obscenity, an act of murder."

"And when the old Samurai killed, Masuto, was that also an act of murder?"

Now Ishido came alive, turning to watch Masuto, who said, "If the Samurai was Samurai and he saw that the swordsman who faced him was weaker or afraid, then he did not use his sword. Do not think of yourself as Samurai, Saunders."

"I would like to," Saunders said, unperturbed. "Twelve years ago, I gave this club a karate room. I have made arrangements for its use tonight—by the two of us. I have explained to the athletic steward that we are both experts and that we intend to explore some movements. Robes and trousers have been placed there, and once we enter that room, we will not be disturbed. I am twenty years older than you, Masuto, perhaps a bit more—so I give you that sporting advantage. I may as well tell you bluntly that once we are alone in that room, I intend to kill you."

"And on my part, I am to kill you?"

"If you can."

"Whether or not I can is beside the point," Masuto said. "I am not an executioner, Saunders, I am a policeman. I do not kill people—not even people like yourself, who have surrendered all claim to being a part of the human race. Nor will I use karate to kill. That would be a betrayal of something very deep in myself."

"What is your alternative, Masuto? You're not even carrying a weapon tonight. Those two men have silencers on their pistols. They could kill you and be out of this room before your body fell to the floor. So it would appear to me that you must accept my challenge."

Masuto looked at Ishido and then at Saunders. Then he stood up. "Very well. Let's begin and get it over with."

Ishido remained at the table. He avoided Masuto's

eyes. The two thin-lipped men in the dark suits also remained at their table, and moving in front of Saunders, Masuto left the dining room, passed through the lounge, and then was directed down a passageway, past a notice that said, LOCKER ROOM. It occurred to Masuto now that there were opportunities to bolt, to make a run for it. Possibly the exit points were covered by Saunders's men, possibly not; yet Masuto rejected the notion. To run now was inconceivable, and once he ran, where would the running stop? He had no intention of attempting to kill Saunders, but neither had he any intention of becoming Saunders's victim. No doubt Saunders was good, but then neither was Masuto an amateur. He was at a point where he had no plans, no scheme—and at such moments he resigned himself to the motion. Let come what would; underneath his Western exterior there was a very ancient fatalism.

They entered the karate room. It was forty feet by forty feet, and without windows. There were two large mats on the polished wooden floor, some hooks for kimonos and trousers, and a row of chairs at one end of the room. It was air-conditioned and intensely lit from above. Only a wall telephone connected it with the rest of the club.

In silence Saunders began to change. I am a middle-aged policeman, confined with a madman who believes he will kill me, Masuto said to himself, and still I do not know whether I shall kill him.

"It's not too late," he told Saunders. "You know you can't be convicted. Games like this are for witless children and madmen."

"And sportsmen." Saunders had dropped his clothes. His body was squarely built, muscular, not an ounce of fat anywhere. He slipped on the trousers and kimono, treading lightly, flexing and unflexing his fingers. "Change clothes, Masuto!"

"Sportsmen," Masuto said with contempt. "Sportsmen who kill old women and young girls."

"What the game brings. Change clothes!"

"I think not," Masuto said. "I am not a witless child. Does your white kimono give you a license to kill? You are stark, raving mad, Saunders. Do you think that the trappings of a karate match will allow you to kill me and go free? You are a pompous, bloated fool. You are sick and full of decay."

With a roar of rage, Saunders launched himself at Masuto, his arm coming around in an outside inward swordhand strike. Masuto pivoted and let the strike pass over him. His own back-fist counterstrike missed. He sprang away, his feet, still in shoes, slipping on the floor, and Saunders was upon him with a driving upward elbow strike, which, if it had connected with the full force of Saunders's body behind it, might well have snapped Masuto's neck. It missed by a fraction of an inch, and Masuto, off balance, tried to find purchase for a shod kick to Saunders's groin. It was bad karate, but he was fighting for his life. Saunders was too quick for him, amazingly quick for a man his age, and a hard, high kick from Saunders connected with Masuto's shoulder, caught him off balance, and flung him to the mat.

For a fraction of a second Masuto was as close to death as he had ever been. He had sprawled on his back without purchase or any continuity of motion that could be turned to his defense and in that fraction of a second when he was defenseless, Saunders could have driven a kick to his throat that would have crushed his larynx and burst the blood vessels in his neck. All this Masuto knew, for in such moments the mind works with incredible speed. Then the fraction of a second passed, the lethal moment was over, and Masuto was able to whip himself off his back and into a crouch. Saunders had not moved. He stood rocklike, his motion only half begun, and then he clutched at his chest, went down on his knees, and rolled over on his back.

Masuto got to his feet and approached the recumbent figure carefully. He was ready for anything from this man, any trick, any device; but the wide open, fixed blue eyes were a valid definition. He felt for Saunders's pulse and could not find it. No question about it, the man was dead.

Breathing deeply, his whole body still trembling, Masuto went to a chair and sat down. He sat very quietly for a minute or two, composing his thoughts—bringing himself together, as he would have put it. Then he went to the telephone. As he suspected, it was an automatic switchboard. He dialed nine, and when the dial tone came on, he called Sy Beckman's number. Sophie answered. "If you want him, the bum is sleeping off a drunk, and as far as I'm concerned, I've had it."

"I want him," Masuto said.

"You can damn well have him."

"How do you feel?" he asked Beckman.

"I'm all right."

"Sy, I'm at the West Los Angeles Country Club. They have a karate room here. I need you as quick as you can make it. Now outside this karate room you may find two gentlemen in dark suits and bulging jackets. You'll know them because they're that kind. They're Saunders's hoods, and very likely one of them killed Rosita. So you can take off the kid gloves, if you feel so inclined. Be quick."

Masuto sat down again. His hands were still trembling. He waited until his hands steadied, and then he called Wainwright at his home and told him what had taken place.

"Damn you, Masao, you killed him."

"No, sir, I did not, and he came very close to killing me."

"What about Ishido?"

"He won't run. Right now I want you over here with the ambulance from All Saints Hospital. I want to get his body out of here and have Sam Baxter do an autopsy before anyone knows he's dead."

"You mean no one knows he's dead?"

"I know it. I presume he knows it."

"Damn it, Masao, you know what I mean. You can't sit on a corpse like that. He's not just anybody. He's Eric Saunders."

"I'm not sitting on it, captain. We—myself and what was Saunders—are in the karate room at the club. I imagine Saunders's two baboons are outside the door, and they're both armed and nasty, and I see no reason to open the door and invite their reaction—since I am not armed. And Eric Saunders, I remind you, was a murderous pig."

"Why didn't you say that in the first place? I'll have a squad car over there in a few minutes—"

"No."

"What do you mean, no?"

"Sy Beckman's on his way. Please, captain, let him take care of it."

"You said there were two of them."

"Let Sy take care of it, please."

"No, sir. I am sick and tired of you two running around like this was your own private vendetta."

"Well, as you wish—"

"Masuto, why do you pull these things on me? I've given you clowns more leeway than any sane chief would give a couple of cops, and now suppose the D.A. comes up with a vendetta killing—suppose he says you went overboard and took the law into your own hands? You know what I mean. How do I answer that?"

"I didn't touch Saunders. He died of a heart attack."

"Then why do you need an autopsy? The bastard is dead. It's over."

"I think he was murdered."

"Oh, no, not again."

"Yes, I'm afraid so," Masuto assured him. Now sounds were coming from outside the heavy door to the karate room, and Masuto said, "I must hang up now. Please hurry."

He went to the door and opened it. Beckman filled the doorway, a man in a dark suit hanging limply from each of his huge hands. He flung them into the karate room, where they lay on the floor, bleeding and moaning. Then, panting, he said, "What do you want me to do with these two loathsome bastards?"

"Cuff them and read them their rights, Sy. Concealed weapons, resisting arrest, and with a little luck, maybe murder one."

"And who's that?" Beckman asked, pointing to Saunders.

"Eric Saunders, alias Stanley Cutler. Very dead—very dead indeed, Sy. My God, what is today?"

"Thursday, all day."

"And it was only last Saturday that we found the skeleton."

"That's right. Is it over, Masao?"

"Almost."

"What's left?"

"A few loose pieces. Odds and ends."

"How come the cops aren't here?" Beckman asked suddenly. "I don't mean us. I mean the real cops, the guys in the blue uniforms?"

"Any moment now. I gave you a head start. I thought you'd want to deal with these two."

"I dealt with them," Beckman said.

15

SAMURAI

It was almost midnight, and the pathology room in the basement of All Saints Hospital was deserted except for Masuto, Dr. Sam Baxter, and Dr. Alvin Levine, the resident pathologist whom Masuto had dragged out of bed and pressed into service. Naked and white and sliced open, Saunders's corpse lay on the table. Baxter, washing his hands, said to Levine, "You don't have to close. Just put him on ice. He'll hold."

"You'll be back tomorrow to close him?"

"Why? He's dead, isn't he? Any damn fool can sew him up. Even a witless ghoul like Masuto here can sew him up. Well?" he demanded of Masuto. "Are you satisfied?"

"With what?"

"With what I told you. Cardiac arrest."

"So you told me. What caused it?"

Levine, bending over a microscope, straightened up,

took a test tube from over a flame, and shook it slightly. "I think I have it," he told Masuto. "You noted the high thyroid level?" he said to Baxter.

"So what?"

"It's triiodothyronine."

"He might have been taking it on prescription."

"Why?" Levine wondered. "He's not the type. Anyway, he took enough to kill him."

"How would it work?" Masuto asked him.

"The amount he had in him might result in a brief illusion of energy, then a very rapid heartbeat—so rapid that the heart muscle forces itself into cardiac arrest."

Baxter nodded. "That's possible."

Masuto went out into the street, and for a few minutes he stood in front of the hospital, breathing the cool, sweet night air. Then, with a deep sigh, he climbed into his car and drove to Bel-Air, to the home of his kinsman, Ishido. The electric gate that guarded Ishido's driveway opened up for Masuto, and the servant who opened the door of the house for him said, in Japanese, "Come in. My master is expecting you."

"It is very late—"

"No, he is expecting you."

In the living room Ishido was pouring tea that had already been prepared. He wore a white gown and black slippers and sat cross-legged by the table.

"Join me, please," he said to Masuto.

Masuto sat by the table and accepted a cup of tea.

"No doubt you come from the hospital, where an autopsy was done on that sick and worthless flesh."

"You condemn a friend."

"We were never friends," Ishido said. "Circumstances drew us together."

"You saved my life," Masuto said. "It incurs an obligation."

"Which you cannot repay."

"Not in this life. Perhaps in another."

"Ah, so—and you, the cold and enlightened policeman, you believe the old way, that we live and live again?"

"Who knows? I believe many things."

"You are a strange policeman, Masao. Yes, I gave the thyronine to Saunders in his food, in his tea, so it is quite true that I have murdered him. But I also saved your life. Or did I? Could you have defeated him?"

"I don't know."

"And now you have come to arrest me?"

"If I had not come," Masuto said, "others would come."

"I understand."

"Do you? I take no pleasure from this. I know of the Samurai only what I have read and what the old folks tell me and what I see in silly films."

"You are telling me, nephew, that I have dishonored my lineage?"

"Worse. You have dishonored yourself. And why did you lie to me about Eric Saunders and Burma?"

"That was not a lie. The man he killed was my friend."

"And so you committed murder for the benefit of Eric Saunders. Come on, uncle, that is too much. This is a moment for the truth."

"And what do you know of the truth? You are an American, Masao. I am something else, beyond your understanding. I could have killed Saunders thirty years ago. The punishment would hardly have befitted his crime. To me, death is not what it is to you. It is easy to die. So I did what I had to do, and it gave me a weapon

177

to hold over Saunders. The whole story is in my vault at the bank. He knew that, so he could not kill me with impunity—and I waited. I let him build his empire, and I waited for the moment to bring him and his empire down in ruins."

"And the moment was tonight?" Masuto asked sardonically.

Ishido smiled. "No, nephew, the moment was not tonight. Tonight I changed my plans. I had no desire to see you die. I seek no sympathy. There is simply a matter of the fitness of things." He stood up now, and he made a slight formal bow to Masuto. "I shall not run away, nephew, but I need a few minutes to prepare for my absence and to change my clothes. If you will wait here?"

Masuto nodded. Ishido went into the next room. Masuto sat cross-legged by the table, staring at the tiny cup of green tea that Ishido had prepared for him.

And then he heard the woman scream, a piteous wail of grief.

Masuto rose and went into the next room. A woman was huddled in a heap on the floor, sobbing. Ishido knelt on a velvet cushion, a bit of incense burning before him and both hands clasping the knife that was buried in his breast.

Masuto helped the woman to her feet and led her out of the room. "He is gone," Masuto told her, speaking Japanese slowly and carefully, "but he departed honorably. Now there are things we must do."